BLOODTHIRSTY BEAUTY

"Hate to spoil your fun, boys, but the party's over," Skye announced as he smashed into the cabin where the new schoolmarm was being attacked.

One man, holding the woman, ducked his head to reach for his gun, only to have her ram her head into his chin so hard that he almost bit off his tongue. Fargo wasted no time with a warning shot. His soft lead bullet poked right into the left eye of the woman's attacker.

None of that seemed to bother the lady. From the look in her eyes as she turned to face her other attackers, this schoolmarm was eager to take on the whole bunch. And Fargo began to get the idea that he had run into a woman a man simply had to respect. . . .

THE TRAILSMAN 79

SMOKY HELL TRAIL

by

Jon Sharpe

A SIGNET BOOK

NEW AMERICAN LIBRARY

PUBLISHER'S NOTE

This book is a work of fiction. Names, characters, places, and incidents either are the product of the author's imagination or are used fictitiously, and any resemblance to actual persons, living or dead, events, or locales is entirely coincidental.

The first chapter of this book previously appeared in
MINNESOTA MISSIONARY, the seventy-eighth book in this series.

SIGNET TRADEMARK REG. U.S. PAT. OFF. AND FOREIGN COUNTRIES
REGISTERED TRADEMARK—MARCA REGISTRADA
HECHO EN CHICAGO. U.S.A.

SIGNET, SIGNET CLASSIC, MENTOR, ONYX, PLUME, MERIDIAN
AND NAL BOOKS are published by NAL PENGUIN INC.,
1633 Broadway, New York, New York 10019

First Printing, July, 1988

1   2   3   4   5   6   7   8   9

PRINTED IN THE UNITED STATES OF AMERICA

The Trailsman

Beginnings . . . they bend the tree and they mark the man. Skye Fargo was born when he was eighteen. Terror was his midwife, vengeance his first cry. Killing spawned Skye Fargo, ruthless, cold-blooded murder. Out of the acrid smoke of gunpowder still hanging in the air, he rose, cried out a promise never forgotten.

The Trailsman, they began to call him, all across the West: searcher, scout, hunter, the man who could see where others only looked, his skills for hire but not his soul, the man who lived each day to the fullest, yet trailed each tomorrow. Skye Fargo, the Trailsman, the seeker who could take the wildness of a land and the wanting of a woman and make them his own.

July, 1861, Colorado Territory.
The ramshackle mining camp of Gouge-Eye,
which boasts of being the roughest town in the Rockies—
and fights for that right . . .

1

"You some kind of sissy, mister?"

Gripping the enameled tinware cup with his massive left hand, Skye Fargo shrugged his muscular shoulders, brushing them with his black hair. The tall man with the full beard lifted his lake-blue eyes from the steaming coffee and the battered pine surface of the bar. He turned to his right for a better look at the halfwit who'd asked the question.

This early on a summer day, the pushy miner standing next to the Trailsman was hard to stomach.

Dressed in the usual garb of patched flannel shirt and baggy wool trousers held up by improvised grass-rope suspenders, the miner wore a bushy brown beard that couldn't hide his lean wolfish face, nor the immense hawklike beak protruding from beneath his beady porcine eyes. His humorless grin showed missing teeth, and the remaining chompers had faded to a combination of yellow and brown that was about the color of fresh runny sheep shit.

Which was a pretty fair description of the stink that wafted Fargo's way. The brawny shoulders and hands, though, showed that this grimy saloon idler could feel safe enough whenever he walked up to strangers and started something.

Fargo exhaled slowly through pursed lips, blowing some of the stink away while reining his temper. "Well, if taking regular baths makes a man a sissy, then I might qualify. Anything else on your mind?"

The oaf shuffled back an inch or two before replying. "It ain't just that. If you was a real man, the kind that gets his due respect hereabouts, you'd start your day with a real eye-opener, a man's shot of forty-rod. You wouldn't sip coffee like some pantywaist."

Fargo allowed himself to quiver a bit and look worried. "Fact is, they didn't have what I wanted," he explained, drawing his words out slowly. "I fancied some tea. In a china cup, with a saucer and sugar and a slice of lemon."

The piglike eyes shifted and the man shot a stream of tobacco juice between Fargo's boots. Sawdust floors were meant for absorbing such abuse. They muffled sound pretty well, too, but not well enough to keep Fargo from hearing telltale shuffles behind him.

When the spitter looked up, anticipation was written all over his grubby face. With another insult or two, everything would be in place. "Tea? You'd try to order tea at the Exchange Saloon? Next thing you know, you'll be looking for a place to squat when you piss."

Fargo felt the silent presence behind him and decided that the time had come to get this over with so he could get on his way.

His left hand rose slowly, until the coffee was at shoulder level. His arm sprang like a bullwhip, to cast the scalding liquid back into the face of the light-fingered gent who had been reaching for Fargo's wallet.

Just to make sure the would-be thief got the message, the Trailsman swung his long right leg back, like a mule on the prod. He didn't need to turn to know what happened, because he felt a satisfying squish as his boot heel struck the tender spot where the unseen pickpocket's legs came together.

Before the stinking accomplice in front of him could get over his surprise, Fargo caught his temple with a roundhouse right. The blow slammed the man's ribs against the bar, sliding him back as his flailing right arm knocked his shot glass and half-drained bottle of rotgut to the floor. He brought up his left for a jab that Fargo deflected. The Trailsman followed with an uppercut that flattened the man's beard and snapped his head back. After that, the gent lost interest in this morning's brawl. He turned and sagged face down on the bar.

The oily bartender had to have been in on this little game. He'd disappeared the moment that the rawhiding started. Now he emerged from the back room with a bung starter, a two-pound wooden mallet used for tapping the kegs of the vile-tasting concoctions they sold as beer and whiskey. When he saw that Fargo was the only one still standing in front of the bar, the saloonkeeper looked astonished. Things hadn't gone according to the script.

Fargo had fallen for this ruse once, years ago. The idea was to start hoorahing any passing stranger who might have money in his hip pocket. While the stranger's attention was occupied by the insults in front of him, a light-fingered partner would approach from behind and lift his wallet. The bartender, who got a cut of the proceeds, would keep things orderly. Usually he stepped in before matters got violent between the stranger and the insulter.

This bartender swallowed hard and gave Fargo a thoughtful look. "I'll not have fighting in here," he announced.

"See anybody fighting? I don't, and I've got pretty good eyes." Fargo stepped back to be sure he was out of the hammer's range.

"You can't just come in here and abuse my good local customers," the bartender proclaimed as he noted one patron scrunched up in the sawdust and the other drooping face-first on the bar top. He stepped forward to lay his bung starter under the bar.

"Likely they are good customers. I'm sure they stay right here to spend most of what they steal."

His hands remaining behind the bar, the round-faced man tried to stay expressionless. "You sure ain't easy to get along with, stranger. You come in here and prod me till I make some coffee. Then you start a fight, and now you're saying my saloon is a den of thieves. I don't rightly know how much more of this I'm supposed to take."

Doubled up in the damp sawdust next to the bar rail, the slender pickpocket began to stir and straighten. Fargo ignored that and kept his eyes pinned to the bartender.

"You'll take your hands off that goddamn scattergun you're fixing to pull up," the Trailsman announced as his hand settled on the grip of his Colt.

But maybe they all really did believe that he was a sissy. Because the bartender seemed to think that he could bring up the sawed-off double-barreled shotgun and cut the stranger in half before the Trailsman could draw his Colt and punch a .44-caliber hole just above the man's button nose.

The bartender was wrong about that. He lacked time to consider that error, since his last act was a reflexive pull on the triggers as he fell back. Fargo had sprung forward with his own shot, so he was crouched against the bar as the twin explosions thundered just overhead.

Double-ought buckshot sliced through the barroom. Most of the lead plunked into the primitive roof, a bunch of skinny poles topped with dirt. Dust and mouse turds rained down through the powder smoke as Fargo started to rise, then noticed some twitching in the nearby legs of the gent who'd started all this with the question about morning coffee.

The Trailsman grabbed the nearest leg and jerked it hard, down and away, slamming the man backward to the floor. Had the surface been anything stouter than sawdust, that would have been enough. But the man twisted one leg free while kicking furiously with the other. With his back to the bar, Fargo didn't have much room for dodging, so he caught one bruising hobnailed boot in his chest. Gasping as he crabbed along the bar, away from those striking boots, Fargo got to the knocked-out pickpocket.

The slender thief was starting to sit up and take notice. He stood up when Fargo grabbed his collar and trousers from behind and straightened. Then he got to fly as Fargo spun around once to gain momentum before launching the man, who seemed almost as light as his fingers.

His husky friend was just starting to stand and reach for his pistol when the pinwheeling pickpocket smashed into his belly. Both went down in a cursing heap of thrashing arms and legs.

Fargo stepped easily to the plank door. It sagged on its leather hinges when the Trailsman shoved it open and surveyed the street.

In this overnight town, the rutted thoroughfare still sported a few stumps. It wasn't just the main street, it was the only street in Gouge-Eye, a collection of thirty-odd raw cabins and tents that bragged on being the roughest mining camp in Colorado Territory, where there was considerable competition in that department.

With big ground-eating steps, Fargo left the saloon and headed for the stable, where his big Ovaro pinto stallion would be waiting in a splintered stall.

Getting out of Gouge-Eye had seemed like a good idea early on this morning, and it sounded even better now. But it would be a day or two before he could leave this hellhole totally behind him.

His job had been to get a mine boiler and hoisting apparatus up here from St. Joseph, Missouri, as fast as possible. Surprisingly, the trip had gone smoothly. By taking the old California Trail up the Platte, then following that river's south fork past Denver City and on up the new toll road into the mountains, they'd made the trip in only six weeks, good time. Too good a time, as it turned out.

Darius Hamilton owned the Morningstar Mine, on the rim of Handcart Gulch two miles above Gouge-Eye. He'd hired Fargo to bring in the machinery. Not expecting the Trailsman to arrive quite so early, Hamilton was out of town and wouldn't be back until tomorrow or the day after. Fargo had arrived two days ago.

Yesterday hadn't been too bad, even for a restless sort like the Trailsman. Every now and again, a man needed to spend a quiet day tending to his gear. His Sharps carbine and heavy army-model Colt revolver got thoroughly cleaned and oiled. He replaced two fraying strings on his custom saddle and soaped it, kneading the leather until it was again fully supple. He had pulled the throwing knife out of his right boot and honed its blade until it would smoothly shave a little patch of jet-black hair off his scarred arm.

Those chores done, he felt ready. But there hadn't

been much to do except wait for Hamilton to show up with the rest of his money.

The local boardinghouse had served a tolerable breakfast this morning, with griddle cakes and fresh eggs. But the place had run out of coffee. So the Trailsman had dropped by the Exchange Saloon. He'd been pleased to see it was open that early, but that was about the best he could say for the place.

Out in the stable yard, the Ovaro awaited. Fargo quickly saddled up and headed out of town and toward the mountains. He climbed a zigzag trail that rose from Gouge-Eye, up through logging slash. Not much was on the mountainside except abandoned prospect holes, and the going was slow and not easy. On a ridge just above timberline, the Ovaro caught his wind while Fargo caught his bearings. A jutting granite rib obscured a wagon road as it twisted down-canyon for five miles to the settlement of Webster, where it joined the toll road up the South Platte into the mountains.

Staying on the broad ridge, Fargo headed on down valley. He rode for a while, watching the trail. It was a few minutes before he glanced again at the valley floor. A plume of dust was rising there. By riding several hundred yards farther for a better view, the Trailsman saw the reason for the dust. The morning stage was churning up that cloud as six lathered horses pulled it toward Gouge-Eye.

Suddenly there was a puff of gray-blue smoke swirling in that tan cloud. A second or two later, the muffled report of a gunshot reached the Trailsman's ears.

While the Ovaro picked his way down the steep hillside, Fargo couldn't do much more than watch what he didn't like to see.

Atop the stagecoach sat the driver, who was holding the reins with one hand and working a long whip with the other. He had somebody sitting next to him, likely a guard riding shotgun.

About a hundred yards up the road ahead of them, where the valley narrowed some, stood a slender man waving a pistol. Now he was firing it again. The driver just whipped the horses some more and headed straight for the robber in the road, while the man next to him shouldered a rifle and prepared to dispatch the would-be holdup man.

The robber in the road scatted out of the way just in time. His accomplices, waiting in ambush, cut loose with their rifles. Bullets from the first barrage caught the guard. One tore open his shoulder as he fired his first, and only, shot. He started to roll and grab something so he could stay aboard. The next heavy bullet caught his other shoulder with such force that the man flew off his perch, landing in the road.

Fargo knew it wouldn't make sense to prod the Ovaro, even though he wanted to. The horse was stepping as best it could to get down across the rocks and slash on the steep slope—any faster, and he'd likely break a leg. They were almost within range now, but that didn't help a lot when he couldn't be sure where the ambushers were firing from. They were just puffs of smoke rising out of the roadside trees as the coach rolled on toward them, rounding a bend to leave Fargo's view.

Adjusting his own course to the coach's, the Trailsman rode across the hillside, still trending down. More shots sounded before he could dismount in some deadfall about a quarter-mile above the road. He pulled his Sharps carbine out of the saddle boot and knelt behind a downed tree. Fargo exhaled slowly to release his building tension.

Slumped back onto the roof of the halted Concord stagecoach, the driver bled profusely from a fist-sized hole in his gut. Another wound, not as big, poured lifeblood out of one shoulder. As the reins slipped from his grasp, one of the robbers ran to the leaders and checked them before they got frightened and bolted.

The three other gunmen stood by the door, ordering the passengers to alight. Fargo studied his options and didn't like any of them. Shooting downhill from four hundred yards could be tricky, although he could certainly get at least three of the four robbers with his Sharps. But the sides of the stagecoach were kind of flimsy. A big slug from his carbine could sail right through a highwayman, then through that wall to penetrate any passenger perched on the other side.

The horse-holder wouldn't be hard to hit, but what if the horses took off at the moment he lost his grip on a cheek bar? The passengers wouldn't much appreciate being saved from robbers only to have their coach roll off a cliff or smashed against a tree.

Fortunately, the masked men were edgy and kept shuffling around as the first passenger stepped down. Judging by his tinhorn outfit, he was a professional gambler fixing to set up shop in Gouge-Eye. The next passenger emerged. Somewhat potbellied and trying to look dapper even though his coat was threadbare, he had to be a merchant. He was followed by two nondescript sorts who could have been anything from professional mining engineers to mountain riffraff.

Two robbers, their guns drawn, stepped back to give the passengers room to start dropping gold watches and coins into a hat, while the third stayed close to the door, as if he were expecting someone else to get out.

Now that two robbers were in the clear, the Trailsman didn't waste time. Fargo's first shot nearly took the short one's head off. He hadn't even started to fall when his companion spun, snapping a round off Fargo's way. The heavy Sharps bullet caught the robber square in the belly. He jackknifed forward and fell to the ground, still doubled over.

Horse-holder wasn't too sure what to do except to sidle in between the team, where Fargo didn't have a shot at him. The robber at the open door reached in and jerked. He got kicked in the face, but now he had a shield—a slender woman, all dressed for traveling with her broad hat, veil, and drab linen duster.

Among the other passengers, Tinhorn must have been through this before. He slipped over to stoop and grab the reins that had been dragging on the ground, so that, come what may, somebody would have control of the coach. Fargo could see him looking for a way to set the brake without climbing up to the driver's bench, where he'd be too exposed.

The remaining three male passengers just stood and looked befuddled while the woman writhed, trying to escape the grip of the robber behind her. After seeing two of his partners gunned down in front of him, the robber was clearly proddy and dangerous, but he was slow in bringing the gun up to the woman's ear.

He had to work at it. His first two attempts to hold her still came up empty, except for such hair as he gathered with his fingernails. As soon as he got a firm grip, he announced that the fun was over and that if they wanted to see her live, they'd best start cooperating.

The woman quieted and stood ramrod-straight, her arms down at her side. Then she hollered, "Go ahead and shoot me."

The shrill voice carried easily to Fargo. He shook his head, trying to make sense of this, while keeping the robber's shoulder—that was all that showed, besides the arm and gun—in his sights. Up in front, Tinhorn whistled. That was enough to distract the robber holding the woman.

Her dropped arm swung back toward the robber's groin. She twisted sideways, ducking the gun that had been at her ear, while the robber doubled over forward. She brought up a knee from somewhere under her spreading skirts and caught the man in the chin. His gun fired into the earth.

The other three passengers ducked while the woman scampered around front to join Tinhorn. Fargo didn't have a bit of trouble shattering the robber's skull with a slug from his Sharps. The hole in front, just above his eyes, wasn't all that much. But there had to be a considerable opening in back, judging by the spray of brains and blood that splattered against the dusty green door of the stagecoach before the man tumbled into the dirt.

Horse-holder must have hoped that this had been enough of a distraction for him to cut and run. Fargo spotted him hauling ass into the woods, twisting and weaving toward wherever they kept their horses. His Sharps barked. The bullet caught the dogging man in his right shoulder, forcing him to drop the revolver. He fell once, too, but hunkered over and kept moving, staying so low amid the brush that a clean shot was impossible.

Finding him wouldn't be much of a problem, if it became necessary. Likely it wouldn't, so Fargo rose and walked over to the stagecoach.

Tinhorn was the only one there who seemed capable of much more than looking dumb and trembly. But he had his hands full with a sobbing woman.

"Thanks, mister," the merchant finally stammered. "Sure glad you happened along when you did."

The Trailsman looked up at the body on the roof and recalled the corpse back down the road before answering. "Wish I'd arrived sooner, in time to do them some good."

Tinhorn came around from the front, shrugging his shoulders, shaking his head, and muttering something about the contrary ways of womankind. "Nice shooting," he complimented, examining Fargo carefully with a practiced eye.

"Something strange about the way I look?" Fargo asked.

"Mean no offense, mister," the gambler quickly replied. "Just wanted to make sure I know what you look like, so that if you happen along into a game I'm in someday, I'll remember to find some pressing business somewhere else." He stuck out a smooth but muscular hand to shake and introduced himself as Porter Rhodes.

While the woman sobbed by herself up front, Fargo caught the other introductions and asked what happened next.

"Well, there's mail aboard, and we were all bound for Gouge-Eye, so I'd just as soon find some way to get us all there," the merchant said while the others nodded in agreement. "Can't be more than a couple miles."

"Doubt the coach is broken," Fargo agreed. "Somebody give me a hand with him." He pointed down the road to the body of the guard.

They hoisted the corpse up on the roof with the driver's, to take them into town for a decent burial. Somebody suggested doing the same for the robbers' bodies, but that got hooted down in favor of dragging the outlaws' remains a few yards into the woods.

Then Rhodes mentioned that once upon a time, when he'd been cleaned out by somebody a little slicker than he was, he'd had to demean himself and take up honest work. Among that was driving a stagecoach. He said he'd try it again, as long as everybody promised to keep quiet about it. That sounded reasonable to everybody except the woman.

She didn't sound reasonable at all when Fargo stepped up to her. "No reason to keep fretting and carrying on now, ma'am. Everything's under control," he consoled.

"I'm not." She kept shuddering and shaking and sobbing, staying put even as Porter Rhodes hooked the reins over the top rail, then climbed up to the driver's seat.

Fargo grabbed her shoulders. "Look, ma'am. You don't have to get back on this stagecoach if you don't want to. But you've got to step aside or you're going to get run over."

The Trailsman should have guessed that a woman who had just shouted "Go ahead" to a man holding a loaded pistol to her ear might not care much one way or another about the prospect of getting squashed by a stagecoach. So when she straightened and started trying to shake his grasp, he spun her and pushed.

He wasn't rough about it, but there was enough force to move her back. Her knees buckled against the big oak tongue. She started to lose her footing and topple backward. Triumphantly, she rocked forward, ready to stand her ground.

Fargo anticipated the move. His big hands swooped under her arms and propelled her lithe body upward. She flailed her thin arms as his grip moved to her waist and he slung her over his shoulder like a sack of flour. Even though he had a vise grip around her knees, to keep her from kicking with any real force, he couldn't say he was enjoying the way her delicate fists thumped at the small of his back. She just might get lucky and land a kidney punch before they got out of the wagon's way.

But in three steps, they were clear. Rhodes looked down. "Got your hands full, mister?"

The Trailsman nodded.

Rhodes released the brake and got a better grip on the reins. "Just remember that, as a gentleman, I feel duty-bound to protect her honor. She was, after all, a traveling companion." The gambler sighed. "Just hope I don't have to."

"Her honor's as safe with me as she wants it to be," Fargo replied, stepping backward and hoping he'd be able to set her down before she gave him any welts or bruises.

"Glad to hear that." Rhodes chuckled before turning. "Gidyap," he hollered to the horses. "You goddamn spavined crowbait, get your worthless asses up the road before I give you to the Utes for their stewpots." He lashed forward with the whip, expertly popping it just behind a leader's ear. The coach lurched up the road.

As soon as it was out of sight, the Trailsman set the screaming woman down, ready to grab her if she took off running.

2

"Who are you? What do you want from me?" the lithe woman asked in rapid-fire words. Standing straight, she trembled like the haft of a throwing knife that had just stuck a pine board. Her youthful face, lean but not harsh, held a mixture of fear and anger behind the torn veil and superficial scratches inflicted by the late road agent who had tried to use her as a shield.

Satisfied that she wouldn't bolt, at least not until she finished collecting her wits, the Trailsman released his grip on her shoulders. "I'm Skye Fargo, ma'am. And I don't want anything from you that you're not willing to give me."

Such chestnut hair as stuck out from beneath her broad-brimmed hat would have bristled if she'd been a cat. Her eyes, an indeterminate hazel or maybe gray, drew into points. "Just what is that supposed to mean?"

Fargo sighed. A trim and athletic gal who could twist and bounce the way she did would be pure joy on a feather bed. The notion had been flitting through his mind—it generally did whenever he met an attractive woman—but he usually did a better job of hiding his feelings when the woman obviously had other matters in mind.

"Let's start over," the Trailsman suggested. "I'm Skye Fargo. I had to wait around Gouge-Eye for a couple days, so I went for a ride. I heard shots, rode over, and saw your stage was getting robbed. You know pretty much what's happened since. And since you didn't want to get back in that coach, I'd be proud to see you on up to Gouge-Eye if that's what you're of a mind to do. Or I'll get you back down to Hall's

Camp or Webster. But I won't leave you alone here in the mountains. Okay?"

She nodded without enthusiasm before looking up. "Mr. Fargo, where's Gouge-Eye?"

How could she not know where Gouge-Eye was? She'd been a paying passenger on the stagecoach. There weren't any stops past that settlement. "It's just up the road a couple miles, Miss . . . ?"

"Excuse me," she stammered, offering a gloved hand. "I'm Florence Trefethen." Her muscled hand gripped his as she continued, "You must think I'm a complete idiot."

That was a very reasonable assessment of what Fargo thought of her after her last question, but he let it slide. She had showed considerable presence of mind during the robbery, when she'd jabbed that highwayman in the balls with a hat pin. A lot of women got awful flustered in such circumstances, even if they had a clear idea where they were going. Florence Trefethen had kept her wits then, even though she was otherwise about as confused as a person could get.

"Ma'am, it does seem curious that you were on the stage that runs to Gouge-Eye and no place else, and now you're acting like you never heard of the spot."

"But I haven't," she protested. "Or I hadn't until we got past Webster, and the other passengers started talking. But I'm almost sure that's where I was supposed to go."

Fargo felt like sitting down, because this was going to take a while. He motioned at a nearby pink granite boulder of a convenient height. She took the hint as he found a less comfortable rock to perch on. "Miss Trefethen, I don't know if you're confused, but I sure am. Just where were you supposed to go and why?"

"I'm not in the habit," she announced, her low throaty voice gaining substance, "of explaining my business to strangers."

"You know who I am," Fargo prodded.

"I know what name you gave," she sniffed. "But I don't know who or what you are. You stopped a robbery. But if you were a lawman, you'd have shown me your badge. Are you a knight that goes around rescuing damsels in distress? Or some drifter that enjoys gunplay?"

"Some call me the Trailsman," Fargo explained. "I get people, sometimes with their goods or their livestock, from here to there. As for gunfights, I don't like 'em or dislike 'em." The Trailsman shrugged. "Sometimes I run into trouble. When I can't skirt it or talk my way out of it, I shoot." He paused. There wasn't much else to say. "Guess that's about the size of it. Now it's your turn."

Florence trembled a bit, then stiffened her back before answering. Fargo had to work at it to listen to her, because he found himself fascinated by the way her bosom pressed against the starched cotton shirtwaist beneath her open duster.

"This spring," she recounted, "just as I was finishing a school term in Iowa, one of the professors I'd had at the state normal school came through town. He showed me a letter from a gentleman in Colorado Territory. They were looking for a schoolmarm in a brand-new town. I'd get to set up my own school, run just the way I'd like to do things. It sounded interesting, and the salary was most attractive. After some correspondence with the chairman of the board of education, I agreed to take the position. They forwarded my fare and some traveling money."

"I see," Fargo muttered, stretching his long legs and shifting so that a bump on the rock would start grinding away at another part of his ass. "What was the name of this town?"

"They said it was so new it didn't really have a name yet," she explained. "All the mail went through Webster. My stage ticket just said 'end of the line.' And that's the place called Gouge-Eye?" She muffled a sob.

Fargo nodded. "That much adds up. Thing is, I can't imagine a town that'd be less likely to support a school. It's nothing but hard cases, pickpockets, drunks, gamblers, fancy gals, with just a sprinkling of working miners. I just spent two days there, and I didn't see any children, none at all. Gouge-Eye isn't exactly what you'd call a family town. I'd call it a stinking hellhole, but there's a lady present. Let's just say that Gouge-Eye is a pretty accurate way to describe the place."

Florence blushed some before choking another sob and trying to smile. "So you don't think the offer was legitimate?"

"I don't know what to think," Fargo confessed. "Who was the gent that wrote the letters?"

She reached for a purse that wasn't there, and got upset. "My purse," she gasped, "my bags. Where are they?"

"You left them on the coach. It'll come back through, and likely they'll still be aboard. If not, well, they'll be at the station up the road. And if some rascal swipes them in Gouge-Eye, I'll tend to him. There's no law there to complain to."

"There's not? Oh, dear, what did I get into?"

"You don't remember anything more about the letters?"

"They were from a Mr. Hamilton," she said, her face growing pale as she glanced around and saw the three robbers' bodies heaped a few yards away.

"Darius Hamilton? Owner of the Morningstar Mine?"

"I don't know about the mine, but that is indeed the name."

Fargo leaned back to mull on that. "He's the gent I was working for, bringing in some mine machinery. He's not up there right now, but he's due back in town any day. I half-expected him to be on the coach you were on. I need to see him to collect the rest of my pay. Sounds like you'd like to see him, too."

Her head dropped. "I don't know. I don't think so," she said. "I feel like such a fool. Here I agreed to teach children in a school that doesn't exist in a town that sounds more like an outlaw camp. I don't know how I could face Mr. Hamilton."

"Think on it another way, Florence. Start wondering where he's going to find the grit to face you. These problems sound like his doing, not yours."

She stood and flexed her shoulders. Noticing how Fargo enjoyed watching her, she modestly pulled the duster around and buttoned it, then glared at him.

He smiled in response, then rose. "Want to head up to Gouge-Eye, or down to Webster?"

She needed her things, so Gouge-Eye seemed sensible, especially after Fargo explained that the town boardinghouse was reasonably clean. But on the other hand, it sounded like such an awful spot, and Miss Florence Trefethen knew she had no future there. But then again, maybe there really were kids and a school, and the Trailsman just hadn't noticed. She stood in the road hemming and hawing until Fargo thought he had matters settled by settling her atop the Ovaro, which he planned to lead up the road.

But then she complained it wasn't ladylike to sit astride, instead of on a sidesaddle. Impatiently, the Trailsman promised not to have her picture taken. He doubted Gouge-Eye boasted a photographer's studio, anyway.

They managed to get along a little better on the road, while she prattled about teaching school and what a joy it was to bring learning to the wilderness, carrying on the grand task of spreading culture, civilization, and suchlike.

Just before they arrived, Fargo got around to asking her about her effective use of her knee on her captor.

"You learn all kinds of tricks," she explained, "when you're in charge of a room full of unruly children."

"But little schoolkids don't grab you from behind and use you for a shield," Fargo protested. "That took some quick thinking on your part."

"Believe me," Florence said, "those robbers did not try anything that my students have not attempted. You must realize that some of them are nearly as old as I, even in an eight-grade country schoolhouse, and that among them were some big, strapping farm boys. Some were even bigger than you are. If I am to maintain discipline, I have to handle them. A hand or knee properly applied . . ."

Fargo winced when he thought about it, and felt almost relieved when the aroma of wood smoke mixed with fresh horseshit and rotting garbage advised that Gouge-Eye was just around the bend.

From the sound of it, Gouge-Eye was more excited

than usual. Angry men milled along the street. Fortunately the livery stable was on their edge of town, so there was a chance to ask some questions before wandering into the tension that crackled in the thin air.

"All that commotion?" the stove-up hostler answered as he shuffled toward a stall while Florence waited up front. "Been some excitement hereabouts, even more'n the usual. Day starts with Slim Boswick and Pugnose Ryan crawling outta the Exchange, both of 'em beat up considerable. Back inside, the barkeep's got a hole atwixt his ears. They're saying some stranger done it. 'Bout the time that folks get a chance to get steamed up over that, then the stage gets robbed a-coming in. Three of the owl-hoots gets killed, but one was winged and run off. We figure they was somehow in on the killing at the saloon. Anyhow, we found that last stage robber, and he's fixing to be the guest of honor at a necktie party. You got here just in time, mister."

Fargo didn't feel like thanking the shuffling stablehand for the information, but did so anyway. He wanted to get Florence over to the boardinghouse after checking at the stage station for her bags—the coach was still sitting over there—but that wasn't going to work. Not if he didn't want to see an innocent kid lynched.

The Trailsman knew for certain that the short blond kid in the middle of the mob hadn't killed the bartender. If the kid had been in on the robbery, he'd stuck damn well to the bushes. He had a shoulder wound, sure enough, but in his left shoulder. Fargo closed his eyes and played the shot through, just to be certain. The shot from his Sharps had hit the fleeing bandit's right shoulder.

"What's going on?" Florence asked.

The Trailsman told her and wondered where the hell she was going to stay safe during the ugly mess that was about to happen. The boardinghouse was on the far end of town. Getting there by going down the street was out of the question, as was sending her by herself. Going around was possible, but the kid would be twisting in the afternoon breeze before Fargo could get there and back.

"That kid had nothing to do with the robbery," Fargo muttered. "He's shot in the wrong shoulder. Besides, I killed that bartender." He quickly added, "In self-defense, of course."

"That's awful," Florence gasped. "Isn't there anything we can do?"

"There is. Just stay by me, no matter what. And I'll warn you now that you won't like this a damn bit."

She bristled at the profanity. "I shall manage, Mr. Fargo."

Most men were willing to step aside for a lady. A few weren't, but Fargo didn't mind shouldering and elbowing when necessary. They pushed to the center of the mob.

Everything was almost ready. The twitching blindfolded kid sat atop a sorrel mare, his hands tied behind his back. Fresh blood joined older red-brown stains at the top of the left sleeve of his faded flannel shirt. His Adam's apple bobbed up and down along his scrawny neck, but at least the noose hadn't arrived yet. It hung ominously from the gantry that protruded from the nearest building, a two-story barnlike log structure that housed the usual shop where they made things out of wood—furniture, coffins, cabinets, wagons, and so forth.

All that remained was for one of the town leaders—they had to be that knot of men close by on horseback—to ride up, place the noose, give the kid his last words, and swat the sorrel.

Fargo felt confident that if he could get the crowd's attention, he could stop the lynching. He tried hollering. In the rumble of the mob, his voice stood out about as much as piss in the ocean.

He leaned down and whispered in Florence's ear. "You're sure you don't want to work here?"

"For a million dollars a year, I wouldn't teach here," she hissed. "How many deaths must I see in one day?"

"You've seen enough," he agreed, "but they haven't." The Trailsman and the schoolmarm stepped into an area clear of congestion, just a few steps away from the sorrel bearing the unwilling guest of honor.

"Haven't seen enough killing?" she asked, straining to make her low voice heard over the rising drone of the crowd.

"No. They never see enough of that. But they haven't seen enough of you, either. Start undoing the buttons on that duster. And that's just the start. Keep taking clothes off till I tell you different."

She bristled and spun to face him. "Mr. Fargo!"

"They'll listen if we can get their attention before they hang the wrong jasper for robbing the stage. I tried shouting."

"Couldn't you just shoot your gun?"

"Gunshots breed gunshots. Lots of lead flying in a crowd, and somebody could get hurt. Just how devoted to civilization are you, Florence? Do you want to stop this before a man gets killed, or don't you?"

Not quite persuaded, Florence bit her lip.

"Look, Florence, I grant it'll ruin your reputation and you'll never get a job teaching school in Gouge-Eye. But not a man here will touch you. I'm siding you."

"I saw what you can do with a gun," she conceded before turning to face the crowd. Standing at Fargo's side, she pulled off her gloves and dropped them into the drab brown linen duster's big pockets. She quickly undid the big buttons on the duster before she slipped it off her shoulders and let it fall into the rutted street. Fargo knelt to pick it up—she'd need it shortly—while she gingerly worked on the imitation-pearl buttons on her ruffled cotton shirtwaist.

So far, she hadn't attracted notice from anyone besides a few slobbering gents in the front, and even they kept glancing back up at the horse. A stir in the crowd advised that someone was approaching from behind them, no doubt a rider to place the noose.

"Hurry," Fargo prodded, helping slip the blouse off her slim but muscled shoulders.

Those muscles showed growing tension while she worked the straps of her chemise across them. "I'm not wearing a corset," she confessed as her pert nipples swelled under the flimsy cloth.

Florence closed her eyes and started to bare her

chest, then hesitated. Now the nearby men wouldn't have noticed if the kid on horseback had sprouted horns, or even vanished. She lifted a bare arm and plucked a hat pin, then canted her head. The hat and veil fell to the ground, revealing her long mahogany hair, piled in a bun atop her head.

That was about all of her Fargo could see, much to his dismay. But from the tautness of the tendons in her graceful neck, he knew she wasn't seeing anything because she still had her eyes closed. Her hands resumed action on the chemise straps. One at a time, she extricated her arms.

Now only her breasts held up the chemise. He thought he heard her mutter something, through clenched teeth, about wishing that she had more to show if that's what she had to do anyway.

The top slipped down, revealing the swelling roundness that defined her cleavage. The Trailsman couldn't see as much of her as he wanted to; he had to watch the crowd, and he knew, from the gapes, the first instant that one rosy areola emerged, followed seconds later by a cherrylike nipple.

Holding that side there for a moment, the school-marm moved her attention to the other side. Her audience was silent, except for some understandable deep breathing that got deeper as she finished slowly tugging the chemise's top down to her petite waist.

Florence's hands moved to the waistband of her full skirt. Fargo grinned and figured the crowd might be ready to listen now. Just to be sure they'd stay mindful, though, he let her get the skirt loosened. Meanwhile he changed his hold on the duster, so that he had it by the collar with his left hand. His right brought up the big Colt.

"Sorry, folks," he announced, "but you've seen all you're going to see today."

"Say . . . what?" hollered one of the front-row drunks.

He extended the duster to Florence. Her eyes were still closed, though, so she didn't notice. She just went on fiddling with her skirt. Now the garment was slipping down, slowly but enticingly, across her sleek hips, the chemise following to reveal some lacy pantalets.

This wasn't going to work, not at all, if she kept peeling off clothes, undulating as she did so, as if she were dancing to slow rhythmic music that only she could hear. The idea had been to get attention so that he could explain how they were fixing to lynch the wrong guy, a kid that hadn't been part of the robbery, who had nothing to do with the bartender's death this morning.

They had attracted attention, sure enough, but it was all on Florence's skirt, which was now settling into a tepeelike ring on the street.

Almost dreamily, she stepped back, out of the skirt, a perplexed Fargo staying at her side. Florence began to fiddle with those pantalets, her only remaining garment. Her breasts, firm and enchanting, bounced and quivered as the lower reaches of her flat midriff came into view, followed by curling tendrils of pubic hair.

Fargo bent down to get next to her ear. He pushed the words out through clenched teeth. "Florence, dammit, we've got their attention." He brought the duster around to settle it on her shoulders.

She brushed it back with one hand while the other slipped the lace farther down, so that most of her important parts showed, with more creamy thigh emerging by the moment. "Mr. Fargo," she muttered. "I'm a schoolmarm. And a very good one. I know when it's time to start today's lesson."

Which was when she got jaybird naked and finally opened her eyes.

"This man here"—she pointed at Fargo while her voice gained volume and authority—"is the one that killed your bartender this morning."

The best that could be said for the situation was that Fargo now had the crowd's attention. He chose his words carefully while she reached for the duster and slowly pulled it around herself.

"She's right. The son of a bitch pulled a shotgun on me. What happened to him is what's going to happen to the first one of you that makes a move for his gun."

The crowd settled some before Fargo continued.

"I'm also the gent as happened to kill three of your stagecoach robbers, and winged the fourth." Toward the rear of the crowd, he could see the gambler, Porter Rhodes, confirming that to the folks near him. The Trailsman let that information seep through the crowd for a few moments.

"He's not the robber I winged," Fargo announced as he pointed back to the horse and its confused rider. "I hit mine in the right shoulder. His wound's in the left."

"You're sure you know where your shot hit?" A loudmouthed disbeliever stared up. Moments later, his florid round face got as pale as a fish's belly when he saw that Fargo knew just where his next shot would go—between the scoffer's ears.

"Party's over, men. Those of you that have jobs better get to them. The rest of you, which is likely most of you, better get out of our way."

A couple of the younger bystanders volunteered to help Florence pick up her clothes. She spurned their offers. One got slapped when he whispered something to her. Fargo didn't hear exactly what, since he was fetching the sorrel, then slicing the rope that held the wounded kid's hands back.

He noticed, though, that heads still turned in her direction as they walked up the street, heading for the livery stable. The almost-victim was still gagged, and Fargo didn't know what to say, except thanks.

"No," Florence said, "it is I who should thank you."

She didn't explain, and the Trailsman didn't push her. Instead, he cut the gag off the kid, who started bubbling all sorts of nonsense. Getting shaken up was understandable, but hell, it was over. Fargo grabbed him by the collar.

"Look, kid. I don't know how you got that shoulder wound. Maybe you really were just cleaning your gun and had an accident. I do know that you weren't the one I shot in the robbery. The other thing I know is that you'd better get your young ass out of here if you expect it to get much older. They already feel cheated. Next thing that comes up, they'll blame you for it."

The kid nodded and muttered more of his gratitude

before hightailing it down the road. If he had a lick of sense, he wouldn't stop at Webster, but he'd keep moving until he arrived in Texas or California or anyplace else that was a long way from Gouge-Eye.

"Why are we stopping at the stable?" Florence asked.

"Much as I admire watching the way that duster moves across your figure," Fargo explained, "it's doubtless time for you to get dressed again. There's as much privacy in a stall here as you're likely to find anywhere."

"Amazing that you think I might want some privacy." Her steps got harder, almost like stomps.

"Then get dressed here. I don't mind, one way or the other." Fargo laughed, trying to keep matters as light as possible. She went on inside. The hostler had been in the crowd, so he knew why she went inside and why he shouldn't follow. He started jawing at Fargo.

"That was sure somethin'," he marveled. "It'll be a story to tell. Trouble is, nobody'll believe it. That this proper young woman just showed up in Gouge-Eye right afore a hangin', an' stood there an' took all her clothes off so as the big man at her side could stop it afore they strung up the wrong jasper. Hell, it sounds peculiar now, an' I just saw it."

"Today's stage left yet?" Fargo asked.

"Won't run until tomorrow," the stable man answered. "No driver, an' nobody was leavin' today anyhow. They'll send up another driver tomorrow to take this one back."

Fargo nodded and wondered why it always took so long for a woman to dress. "Any place where the lady could stay?"

The hostler scratched his graying head. "If'n she hadn't done what she just did, she could stay at the boardinghouse. But it's just for proper sorts, which she sure ain't now. She don't really strike me as no soiled dove, neither, so the town cathouse is likely out. Got a tent, mister? An' a way to guard it so as she won't get pestered?"

Fargo mulled on that, then asked about the hayloft right behind them.

"You're welcome to it, if she don't mind sleeping

over a stinkful stable. Hard to get help around here to clean the stalls. Those gents as are willin' to do any honest work'd rather shovel rocks than shit. Can't say as I blame 'em, but it means the place don't get cleaned out as often as it ought."

Before he could complain some more, Florence sashayed out, looking as proper as a traveling schoolmarm ought to look. She also had that teacher look in her face, as though she'd just caught Fargo dipping a girl's braids in the inkwell when he ought to have been memorizing his hornbook.

"Mr. Fargo," she proclaimed, "I see that the stagecoach has yet to leave today. You will escort me to it, will you not?"

"I'd be proud to," Fargo said. "I'll even escort you down to Webster, where there's less chance of you being bothered. But I can't do it today."

"And why not?"

He explained. She asked about rooms. He mentioned the hayloft. She inquired about meals. He told her he had some victuals he could cook over a campfire if she didn't know how. She told him he could go to hell, except she called it perdition, then spun on her heels and stomped away.

Fargo easily caught up. He grasped her shoulders and turned her to face him. She reached up deliberately and firmly pushed his hands off.

"You are not my keeper, Mr. Fargo. I am a grown woman. I do not require or request your company or your assistance. I am perfectly capable of finding my own lodgings until I can book passage out of here. Leave me alone."

"You're sure of that?" Fargo asked, stepping back, as though the icy tone of her husky voice were strong enough to push him away.

"Absolutely positive." Florence turned again, as precisely as a drilling soldier performing an about-face. She marched toward the stage station, no doubt to find her baggage.

3

Without much better to do during what promised to be a tedious summer afternoon, Fargo legged it up the mountainside to the Morningstar Mine. The unhurried two-mile uphill walk dispelled most of his tension, although he still felt somewhat edgy. The men he'd hired to help bring the boiler up to Gouge-Eye still had some pay coming. He'd trusted them and they'd held up their end of the deal. They trusted him, and they hadn't seen all the money they'd been promised.

He knew he'd be proddy if he'd been in their situation. As a matter of fact, he mused, he was in the same boat with them, since Darius Hamilton owed him money, too.

But they appeared to be taking this enforced interlude in stride. They were helping the mine's regular crew install the boiler and hoisting machinery at the new headframe above the collar of the shaft that plunged into the rock.

Several of his trailhands greeted Fargo with backslapping grins and only one complaint: the next time that he was with a pretty lady who wanted to take her clothes off in front of a crowd of men, could he please arrange matters so that they were part of the crowd? News traveled fast; some of the teamsters must have brought the story up from town.

Fargo finally found Jake Watkins, the mine foreman, over in the toolroom. He was cussing out the blacksmith for not putting better edges on the drill steels.

"It'd be one goddamn thing if them bits was bein' driven by a machine, like you seem to think, you shithead. But it's another thing entire because there

34

ain't no such machines. Our boys gotta hammer and twist for every miserable inch of hole they get, and they get a hell of a lot more drilling done when they got sharp steel. You fuck up once more, and you can trade jobs with one of the muckers. Good blacksmiths can be tough to find, but any swingin' dick out there could do as good a job as you've been doin'.''

Watkins finished on that with a discussion of the surly smith's probable ancestry, mostly sheep and turkeys and other animals renowned for their stupidity. Then he had to catch his breath before he had time for the Trailsman.

"My men are getting paid for the boiler work, aren't they?" Fargo finally asked.

"Is a pig's prick pork? Ol' Hamilton left instructions afore he left, told me to hire a crew for puttin' in the machinery. You're crew'll do as good as any, I reckon, an' they're gettin' paid regular for this. When the big boss gets back, you'll all get the money that's comin' for haulin' that out here. Like I told you when you got here, nobody figgered on you makin' such good time."

"When's he supposed to get back?"

"Most any old time, I reckon. Mayhaps there's somethin' in today's mail that'll say more. Ain't had time to look at it yet." They left the sullen chewed-out blacksmith and strolled over to the mine office.

Calling it a shack would have been bragging some. Watkins pawed through some papers atop a flimsy two-legged table whose other side was nailed to the wall. "Here's a letter from Hamilton," he muttered, and pulled out a belt knife to slit open the envelope.

Fargo stepped back to allow the strapping gray-haired foreman some privacy.

Watkins mumbled a bit, then squinted at the fly-specked brewery calendar that hung behind the table. "Tomorrow," he said. "Mr. Hamilton's coming back on the stage. He and his boy was over to South Park, lookin' at some diggings there. Catch him when the stage rolls in, less'n it gets held up again, and you'll get paid up. He's real square about that, damn decent, as a matter of fact."

"Never said he wasn't," Fargo replied. "Hate this waiting around, that's all."

"Well, I got work to do. If'n you wishes to hire on here so as to keep yourself busy, just say the word." He scuttled out the door and started hollering at the men who were wrestling with the massive boiler, trying to set it on a rockwork foundation that looked like a short stone-walled house that could use a roof.

Glad he hadn't nodded at the job offer, Fargo strolled down the hill. He studied on how to while away what was left of today, get through the evening and night, and hope tomorrow's stage arrived early. In any town except Gouge-Eye, he might have welcomed this chance to visit the saloons and sample what passed for whiskey. But this settlement held too damn many worthless fools who'd take up any excuse for a fight. Fargo figured he could handle whatever trouble came up, but why the hell did trouble have to come up so damned often here? Drinking in Gouge-Eye was about as relaxing as walking a tightrope in a windstorm.

But, hell, there was only an hour or so of sunlight left. That'd be enough time to fetch a bottle and wrap himself around some dinner at the boardinghouse. Then he'd get comfortable in his room. And if the old gal that ran the place objected to his drinking, he'd move to the hayloft and carry on. If ever there was a place to inspire a man to solitary bouts with a bottle, he was in it.

Not that it made much difference—tomorrow's stagecoach would arrive when it got here, regardless of any timetable—but Fargo figured he might as well ask about the schedule, since he had to pass the stage station to get to the boardinghouse.

The place was locked up for the day. He rattled the door, just to be sure, and began to turn around. But something didn't seem right. There were sounds, muffled sounds, maybe coming from inside. He halted and spun again, pressing his left ear to one of the panes of glass that formed the slab-walled building's only window.

An indistinct intermittent drone was all he heard, like heavy breathing. No, there was more, perhaps something soft rubbing against wood. Fargo considered smashing out the glass to let himself in. He decided he'd try that if his belt knife couldn't manage to spring the primitive latch on the door.

It was shameful, using such a cheap lock for a building where they sometimes stored folks' valuables and baggage overnight. What was more shameful, though, was what Fargo saw after he padded through the shadowy front room to the room in back.

He had to peer through the minuscule slit that remained because they hadn't quite pulled the door shut, and the only light came through the cracks between the wall planks. But he didn't have a bit of trouble figuring out what was going on.

Florence Trefethen had her clothes off again. Only this time, he doubted she'd been the one to take them off. She was twisting and heaving at a considerable clip, but even at that, she wasn't making headway worth mention against the four men in the room.

One, the husky gent who'd tried to lure Fargo into that argument about morning coffee, squatted with his back to the far wall. He had one of Florence's limber arms twisted in a half nelson, and his other paw was clamped over her mouth.

Two others perched closer, each holding onto a foot that they twisted outward, so as to force her legs apart. The standing man, who was shucking his trousers, must have won the toss for who went first. Railthin, he had his back to Fargo. Even in this dim light, his long, spidery fingers were visible as he dropped his pants.

Fargo's suspicion that he was looking at this morning's pickpocket got confirmed when the lean man whispered that he'd taken a nasty kick before breakfast, and now he was going to make sure that all his plumbing still worked.

Fargo silently drew his Colt and loudly kicked the door open. "Hate to spoil your fun again, boys, but this party's over, too."

Slim hadn't waited for the Trailsman's announcement. As soon as he heard the door crash open, he'd ducked for the gun belt on his trousers. He started to turn and come up with it, only to find Fargo's boot knocking out his two front teeth. Blood pouring from his mouth, he rocked backward, rolling against one of the foot-holders so hard that the man lost his grip. Freed, Florence's leg thrashed. Her heel caught him in the cheek, knocking his head against Slim's with a thunk.

Taking advantage of that distraction, as well as Fargo's unwillingness to fire in such dim light at a target so close to the woman's head, Pugnose reached for his gun. Florence immediately rolled, releasing the pressure of his twisting hold on his arm. She was going for a big bite of his thigh while her free arm tried to chop his gun arm.

Pugnose didn't let that hamper him, though. He managed to pull his Remington out of his holster just before he felt compelled to duck, seeing as one of Fargo's bullets had just whistled by, no more than an inch from his ear. When his head went down, Florence rammed hers up, into his chin so hard that he bit off the end of his tongue, a slimy morsel that landed on her bare back.

The other foot-holder got over being surprised. He grabbed a chunk of the dirt floor and heaved the clod at Fargo's face. The Trailsman avoided his instinct to duck, but he couldn't help blinking. He had to keep blinking, too, because the damn clod had exploded into a little cloud of eye-scratching dust.

Fargo stepped back, to block the door against any escapes, and tried to get a handle on the scene. The dirt-thrower was crawfishing across the room, over to his two befuddled companions, who still hadn't figured out what to do about the flying feet that kept coming at them. Pugnose—maybe he'd go by pug-tongue if he lived through this—wasn't too worried about Fargo. His troubles came from a closer source, the fierce gal that was biting his thigh while her left hand, its fingers locked straight, was jabbing at his throat.

Pugnose went to pistol-whip Florence, since that looked like the only way to settle her down. This time, Fargo didn't bother to shoot wide. The soft lead bullet poked into his left eye, spraying Florence with blood on its way in. On the way out, it expanded and splattered whatever brains Pugnose had possessed against the back wall.

Finally free of any man's grasp, Florence sat up while Fargo faced down the three men huddled on the floor. Slim's eyes flitted at his belt knife, within easy reach.

"Don't even think about that," the Trailsman cautioned. He lowered the muzzle of his Colt just a bit. "Guess kicking you in your cods didn't teach you any manners. Tell you what, Slim. You reach for that knife, and I'll blow a hole between your legs, right where your pecker is now."

Slim slowly settled back. The bigger one of his companions got mouthy, though. "What call did you have to bust this up? She was askin' for this, you know."

Before replying, Fargo glanced over at Florence. She'd clutched her voluminous skirt over herself as she sat on the floor, just staring. Whatever else was on her face was impossible to make out. This room was dim to start with, the powder smoke didn't help, and such light as there was came from behind her.

"Do tell," the Trailsman finally answered, trying to keep his temper in check. "Just how did she ask? Did she wear a sign that said, 'Please hold me down and fuck me while I struggle as hard as I can against you'? Or did she walk up to you and ask if you gents would be so kind as to take turns poking at her while you held her legs apart? I've spent considerable time around Miss Trefethen, and I don't remember her ever making that kind of request."

Maybe the mouthy asshole couldn't see either the ominous expression on Fargo's face, or the way he held the Colt. Either should have warned him to keep his mouth shut.

"You know what I means, mister. She done took all her duds off, right in front of everybody. If that ain't askin' for it, then what was she up to?"

"All she was asking for was your attention, shithead, and there wasn't any other way to get it. That's because you're too fucking dumb to listen to anybody that's trying to be reasonable with you." He turned. "Miss Trefethen?"

"Yes." Her voice was like steel rasping against steel. "Could you help me out here?"

"Of course." Not quite so much steel this time.

"Borrow Pugnose's knife and cut some blinders and gags out of his trousers, which he won't ever need again." Fargo paused. "While you're at it, slice up some long strips, too."

There wasn't any simple way to teach these louts some manners, not without just clubbing them where they sat. The notion had its appeal, but Fargo had qualms about it. For one thing, that kind of rude behavior would get Florence's hackles up, and the feisty woman already had enough reasons to be pissed off at the world in general and perhaps Fargo in particular.

Florence managed to find her duster and pull it on. She stood in a corner with Pugnose's Remington. Standing against the other wall, the men waited their turn to get their hands tied behind their backs, then gagged and blindfolded, before they were shoved down to the dirt floor, to get their ankles tied together. Fargo tied strips of dirty wool between their wrists and ankles, so that they couldn't stand up. It was the best he could do to keep them out of the way in a town that didn't have a jail.

"I'd like some privacy while I dress, Mr. Fargo," Florence announced while he trussed up the last one.

"These gents won't be watching, and I can step to the outer room."

She pointed toward Pugnose, whose remaining eye leered toward her, and shuddered as she spoke. "I can't. Not in here. Not with him."

"He's just meat, that's all." Fargo shrugged. "Use the outer room, then. But there's a window. You might draw another crowd if anybody happens by."

"Maybe it has curtains." She stepped past him and slammed the door behind her.

Fargo waited a discreet interval before gingerly opening the door. She'd covered the window with her duster, although it was nigh dark outside. Enough light crept through to reveal her buttoning her shirtwaist.

Once they got out in the twilight, it was obvious that

the four men had to work for what little they got from Florence. Her blouse was torn and missing buttons, and her skirt showed similar evidence of rough handling.

"I suppose, Mr. Fargo, that you're going to tell me that you were right, that I had no business going anywhere by myself here after my performance earlier today."

Fargo adjusted his pace to match hers as they walked, more or less toward the boardinghouse. "No. If you haven't figured that out by now, there's no sense in my telling you anything."

Her regular steps continued. "And you're going to ask how I ended up in that predicament."

"No. I already know. You went down to see about your bags. The regular station agent was doubtless out running errands or whatever, so he had one of the town idlers watch the office. I don't know which one of those men it was, but he had his friends in there with him. They hoorahed you when you asked about your bags, wondering why you'd want your clothes when you looked so pretty without any. Then they got rough about it."

He sensed her nod before she spoke. "And so the great Trailsman again rescues a damsel in distress. The same one, twice in one day. Is that some kind of record?"

"Will you get off your high horse?" he exploded. "Look, that brassy show you put on downtown might have gone on longer than I thought it needed to. But you sure helped me out of what could have turned mighty ugly if I'd tried to stop a lynching on my own. You helped save a life."

"And I just watched you take another."

"Before he could either pistol-whip you or shoot me. Pugnose made his own damn decision to die hard and sudden. He decided on that a long time ago, back when he took up rawhiding strangers to help his buddy pick pockets. His death bullet would have come sooner or later, and if I didn't fire it, somebody else would have."

Her stride slowed and faltered, although she kept

moving. "Perhaps," she conceded. "Where are we to dine tonight? Where am I to sleep?"

"Hadn't given that much thought, since you told me you could handle that all on your own."

"Maybe I was wrong."

"Maybe you weren't. Don't sell yourself short, Florence. The best I could find you was the loft at the stable, and dinner would be catch as can."

"What do you expect in return?"

"You to get back to Iowa without any more damage."

"That's all?"

"That's all I expect. What I'd like is another matter entire."

She huffed, then grabbed his arm. He turned to face her, although it was too dark to matter which way he looked.

"See here, Mr. Fargo. I'm as grateful as can be for what you've done for me today, and I'll live through what you've talked me into doing today. And whether I like it or not, I need a man at my side in this miserable town. And you're the only man who's seemed interested in anything besides swiving me."

"Swiving you?"

"Schoolmarm talk," she explained. "It's an old word they used centuries ago. It means the same as . . . Well, you know, the 'F' word. But it sounds so much nicer."

"I see. Now, you were driving at something before I raised my hand and asked my dumb question. What's the point of all this, Miss Trefethen?"

"The point is that I believe you are for hire, and I need your services."

"I'm for hire now, and ready to go as soon as Darius Hamilton gets here with my money for the last job. But we'd better settle on just what services you want, and just how you figure on paying for them."

The livery stable, announced by its aroma, loomed up before them in the darkness. Fargo opened a side door and lit a lamp in the front office before she continued.

"I want you to guard me this evening, and to escort

me to Webster tomorrow, perhaps as far as Denver City if necessary."

Fargo grinned. "Be proud to guard you real close tonight. Don't think there's a man in town with grit enough to bother my bedroll if I'm in it with you."

She blushed but didn't get flustered. "Our relationship will be strictly business, Mr. Fargo. Which means you will be paid in cash for services."

"What kind of services?" he provoked.

"I am not some slattern or trollop, Mr. Fargo, despite what you may think after I cooperated with you today."

"I know, you're a schoolmarm."

"That's right. So I might offer my professional services. Perhaps you could use some tutoring: Latin, higher mathematics, literature, fine painting—"

Fargo interrupted her. "Cash would be just fine, Miss Trefethen."

"My resources are limited," she cautioned.

"Nobody has unlimited resources," Fargo replied. "I'm sure we can work something out in the morning."

Their conversation became more sociable after Fargo fished some canned tomatoes and jerky out of his saddlebags, back by the Ovaro's stall.

She talked about some kids full of devilment. "They do make it hard. And at first, I was so scared to stand up in front of the room. Just the thought of that frightened the daylights out of me. I had nightmares and fretted constantly."

"You don't seem so shy now about standing in front of a crowd."

She blushed and giggled, or else she was so nervous that her laugh just sounded that way. "That's why I wanted to thank you after I . . . Well, you know, when we stopped the lynching."

"That's right. You did say you should thank me. But you never said why."

She leaned back and took a deep breath, then sat up straight and stared at him. "Because I still had that fear of standing in front of a crowd of strangers. I have these awful dreams, where I'm totally nude and have to stand before an audience. I wake up terrified, trembling, wet with perspiration."

"Seems odd to be grateful that your worst nightmare came true."

"Can't you see, Skye? I shall never have such nightmares again. I did it. I stood there and took off my clothes in front of a crowd of total strangers, and then said what I had to say. And I didn't melt or get petrified. I don't believe I even blushed."

Fargo sat up straight, shaking off a cloud of hay dust and mold. "No, you didn't blush. I don't recall that you even sprouted goose pimples. And I guess that explains why you took off more duds than you really needed to, which surprised hell out of me."

"Skye, can't you express yourself without profanity?"

"Only with difficulty. Most folks out here don't listen worth mention unless you spice up your talk."

"I noticed how much trouble it can be to get people's attention when you have something to say."

They both laughed for a moment, until a yawn caught up to her. Fargo stood and stretched, then knelt and began to untie the rope that kept his bedroll in a roll.

"You've had a long, rough day, Florence. You make yourself comfortable in here."

"Where will you be?" she asked, a bit of fear creeping into her low voice.

"Hard to say. Likely down at the boardinghouse."

"You can't leave me by myself in this town again. Besides that, I've hired you to guard me."

Fargo stepped over to the ladder before turning to answer her. "Look, Florence. I'll pull the ladder down, so nobody can crawl up here to pester or abuse or trifle with you tonight. I'll be damned if I stay here and sleep in this scratchy, moldy hay when there's a comfortable bed I've already rented. You've got my bedroll, and even if I've seen a lot of you today, you haven't shown sign one that you want company tonight."

She started to splutter some interruption, but he went on. "I'm just a man with normal instincts. If I'm in this damn stable, I plan to be comfortable, which means in my blankets. Which means sleeping at your side. Which means I'd be in a lather about that stuff you call swiving. Which means you'd get surly as a she-bear if I followed my instincts, and I'd get even crosser if I got so tempted and couldn't. So let's stay on each other's good side, which means staying apart tonight."

The old gal at the boardinghouse looked funny at Fargo when he insisted that he be allowed to take a rickety ladder to his room. But she must have caught the icy glare in his eyes, because she didn't argue.

4

Skye Fargo had never felt any particular temptation to set up shop somewhere as the town bully. But he understood why some men might enjoy that role as he and Florence walked up Gouge-Eye's street toward Darius Hamilton's house.

Even the hardest-looking gents were stepping lively when they stepped aside to make way for the couple. The whispers that floated through the dust on this summer morning were damn near entertaining. "Look the other way, darn it. That jasper done shot two fellers just for glancin' at her." "He kilt the bartender at the Exchange just for not fetchin' him his coffee fast enough." "Don't get crossways with that big galoot. He plugged Pugnose, then horsewhipped and hog-tied the rest of that crew. Left 'em all trussed up in the stage depot all last night."

Hamilton's house sat on the far edge of town, almost in the trees. Like most mine-owners, he put his home as far away as conveniently possible from the noise and grime of his mine. It was built of logs, but its timbers had been squared on at least two sides. Behind the full-length porch, it sported more real windows then the rest of the houses in town put together.

Florence stared at the windows as they walked up. "There's no woman in that home," she told Fargo.

"Why do you say that?"

"Those windows are filthy. So are the curtains behind them."

Fargo felt a bit chagrined at not noticing that for himself. But he filed that observation away as something he should remember. Someday such information might come in handy. He started to rap on the finished door, then saw a brass knocker and thumped it.

Hamilton answered the door, pretty well confirming Florence's surmise. He was a big man, close to Fargo's height, although considerably older. The age showed in the graying of his neatly trimmed beard, as well as in a paunch that made suspenders a necessity for holding up his brown broadcloth trousers.

"Mr. Fargo." He extended his hand. "And you would be Mrs. Fargo?"

Florence stepped back, pulling her gloved hand off Fargo's elbow. "No, sir. I am Miss Florence Trefethen."

Hamilton looked confused for a moment, then remembered. "Oh, yes, of course. The schoolmarm we engaged. I must apologize for being out of town on business when you all arrived. I just had no way of knowing that everyone would be coming so soon, or I'd have changed my schedule." He motioned toward the parlor and asked how they liked their coffee.

Once the pleasantries were out of the way, Hamilton started talking business. "Mr. Fargo, Jake met me when the stage came in. I sent him back up to the mine with instructions to pay your men what they have coming for the trip. Any of them that want to stay on our crew are welcome to." He picked up a small leather bag. "Your final payment is here." It was satisfyingly heavy with gold coins as Fargo stuck it in his coat pocket.

Hamilton leaned back in his overstuffed chair. "I've only been back a couple hours, and already I've heard all manner of stories about both of you." Florence fidgeted at that, so he turned his attention to Fargo. "Mr. Fargo, I know you're the Trailsman, a man that never stays in one place for long. But I'm wondering if you'd consider staying here for a spell."

"In Gouge-Eye?" Fargo's tone made it obvious he'd rather book a room in hell.

"Of course." The mine-owner sat up straighter, and his arms started waving as he spoke, his hands drawing patterns in the air. "Mr. Fargo, you've no idea how difficult it is to run an honest enterprise in a place with no law. You could be the law here. In just a few days, you stopped the gang that has been robbing our stages. You halted the badger games at the Exchange Saloon. You put an end to Pugnose Ryan, and his hangers-on were just leaving town when I arrived. Good riddance, if you ask me. That Slim was a pickpocket, and the other two were thieving trash we had to fire from the Morningstar. Anyway, people respect you here. This could become a decent town if you were its lawman."

Fargo tried to envision himself wearing a star. That part wasn't bad, but he'd seen what came with it: petty small-town politics, forced confrontations with surly strangers, being on duty twenty-four hours a day, coping with the payoffs from the whorehouses, covering up the indiscretions of the town fathers.

"It's a flattering offer, and I thank you for it, Mr. Hamilton, but you were right the first time. Staying in one place for very long isn't my style."

Fargo rose, more to stretch than to leave. Hamilton's pleading look made the Trailsman return to his chair while the mine-owner turned to Florence.

"Miss Trefethen, when do you intend to open the school term? I need to know, so we can get one built."

"Never," she replied calmly. "Not here, anyway. After what I did . . ."

Hamilton chuckled as he eyed the swells and dips in her pale linen dress. "There was considerable talk about that, Miss Trefethen. And I have to confess that I'm sorry I missed that show. But I admire a woman with spunk. You're the strong kind we need to run a school here."

Fargo interjected, "Just who would be going to school here? I didn't see any kids around town. Matter of fact, I haven't seen any womenfolk at all hereabouts, aside from the fancy gals at the saloons."

Hamilton sighed. "I guess I'd best tell you the whole story. Perhaps you'll change your mind."

His wife, Lydia, had died last summer from what sounded like mountain fever. They had only one child, a boy named Charlie, who'd just turned fourteen. Hamilton was a wealthy man, getting wealthier by the day, and he wanted the boy brought up right.

"He'd been schooled when we lived in Missouri.

When we came out here, Lydia taught him at home. I kept thinking that Gouge-Eye would develop some, and maybe change its name to something decent, so that men would bring their families here and we'd get a regular school. Then Lydia passed away. Charlie's a good kid, but I can't mind him all the time, so he often has the run of the town. Is this any kind of place for a growing boy? I decided that we needed a school, even if he'd be the only student at first. If necessary, I'm willing to stand all the costs of a school. So I advertised for a teacher."

Florence spoke up. "False advertising. All the letters were from Webster, not here."

The mine-owner shifted uncomfortably. "A town named Webster would be considerably more attractive to a good teacher than a mining camp called Gouge-Eye, don't you think?"

Florence conceded that Webster had a good name in her line of work. But she repeated that she had no intention of staying around Gouge-Eye any longer than it would take for her to get her gear together so that Fargo could escort her down to Webster, a somewhat more civilized place, to catch the stage back to Denver and points east. She rose and turned, heading for the front door.

Hamilton caught up and stood before her, blocking her exit. "Miss Trefethen, I'm truly sorry. Maybe I'm too concerned about my son's upbringing. I just didn't know any other way to get a teacher here. I suppose I am guilty of luring you here under false pretenses. Would you allow me to provide your return expenses? I know I'll never be able to make it up to you entirely for what's happened because you came here, but I don't want you to be out any money on my account."

From the way her back got stiff during Hamilton's request, Fargo was sure Florence would tell him to take a long walk off a short pier. But she relaxed before answering. "It's not necessary, Mr. Hamilton. I am a grown woman. I should have investigated further before accepting your offer. One learns by experience, though, and this entire venture has been educational, to say the least."

"So you're set on going back, and you've hired Mr. Fargo to escort you?"

She nodded. Hamilton got a defeated look and shrugged his shoulders. Then his face brightened. "Miss Trefethen, I'd like to discuss something with Mr. Fargo. You're welcome to stay—in fact, I'd prefer you did—because you've already engaged him, so you might be involved."

With an exasperated look, Florence returned to her chair and sipped at her cold coffee, laden with cream and sugar. Hamilton stopped at a humidor atop an end table and fished out two panatelas. "Do you mind, miss?"

"It's your home," she said resignedly.

Fargo accepted the cigar as well as Hamilton's lit match. They had the room clouded up before Hamilton made his offer.

"It's like this, Mr. Fargo. I don't know what to do with Charlie, now that there won't be a teacher here. He hangs around up at the mine sometimes. Maybe it would be good for him to take up some honest work there, but he's the boss's son. It wouldn't work right. He'd either get pampered or stepped on. I can't just let him run loose around town—not this town, anyway. If he didn't get shot or stabbed, he'd pick up all sorts of bad habits."

Hamilton paused and looked at his cigar. "Not to say that he won't acquire a few bad habits someday. But let him take up whiskey and cigars and whatever when he's closer to being a man who has to make decisions and live with their consequences."

Fargo nodded. "Sounds reasonable enough. You don't want to nursemaid your boy, but you'd like somebody to keep an eye on him. You'd like him to get some more education, too."

"That's right," Hamilton agreed. "Now, I didn't know you were in the escorting business until Miss Trefethen brought it up. Mr. Fargo, I'd like you to take Charlie to St. Louis and enroll him in the Covenant Academy there."

"That's a fine school," Florence pointed out.

"It certainly is," Hamilton continued. "I don't like

the idea of sending the only family I have away. But if I can't get a school going here, I don't see as I have much choice, unless I want him to grow up like the riffraff here."

Fargo stood and stretched, feeling mildly dizzy, the way he did every time he accepted a cigar to be sociable.

"Mr. Hamilton, that all sounds sensible. But he's not some baby. Why not just put him on the stage for St. Louis? If he's fourteen, he's big enough to handle that."

Hamilton stood and stared at Fargo with big brown eyes. "Because stagecoaches get robbed, as you both well know. Because an impressionable young man could fall in with the wrong sort. Tinhorns and the like look awfully exciting to a growing boy, especially when they offer him grown-up whiskey and a fling with the fancy gals. Lord knows, he'll run into all that soon enough. But let him get dry behind the ears first. I want him to get to St. Louis with his mind on learning something, on making something out of himself, instead of with a whiskey habit and a gambling habit and a yen to visit the sporting houses."

The Trailsman couldn't help but smile a little, enough for Hamilton to see.

"I know, Mr. Fargo. You're likely not some paragon of virtue. Nobody would confuse you with a preacher or a Sunday-school teacher or a temperance lecturer. But I do know that you're a man of your word. That if you took the job, I could trust my only son to your care, and that you wouldn't let him go astray."

Florence stood and joined them. "I can't see how that would interfere with escorting me to Webster."

No, it wouldn't, Fargo thought. And having an extra person around would reduce any chance that he and she might get around to sharing his bedroll. The more Fargo looked at Florence, the more trouble he had shaking off that notion. Damn, it would be fun, the way she could move that lithe, limber body that still had curves where women ought to.

The Trailsman looked back to the mine-owner, who

stood there expectantly as Fargo continued pondering the offer. Hamilton would doubtless pay well. And there was always work around St. Louis for when this job was done, whereas lining up work in Colorado Territory was a catch-as-can proposition, depending on how well the hit-and-miss mines were paying. Sometimes a gent that looked flush would hire you, and by the time the job was done, he'd be busted again.

"Mr. Hamilton," Fargo finally announced, "I'll study on it. I can't say for sure until I get to talk to your boy. If he and I don't get along, then you haven't got enough money, and you'll never mine enough gold, to pay me for making such a trip. But if he's a kid I think I can ride with, then I'll take your offer. Where is he? I want to talk to him without him knowing what we're up to."

Hamilton stepped back, relieved. "Like I told you, Mr. Fargo, he's a good kid. A little rambunctious from time to time, like all boys, but overall . . . Well, I'll miss him." He choked a bit before continuing. "I don't believe you'll have a bit of trouble making friends. As best I know, he's up at the mine right now, likely making a pest of himself."

As he stepped toward the door, Fargo heard Hamilton explain to Florence that he had business in town. She was welcome to stay there as long as she wished, though, being as he understood why she might not want to be wandering about unescorted.

The Trailsman didn't have any trouble finding young Charlie Hamilton at the Morningstar Mine. It was lunchtime. The men underground would stay below for the meals they'd carried down in old lard buckets at the start of the shift. The topside workers weren't eating, though. They were standing in a circle, hollering and making bets.

Fargo elbowed his way through to catch a familiar spectacle. A barrel-chested man with a full beard was on top, firming up his grip on the kicking, wriggling kid underneath. He had to be Charlie Hamilton. Stretched out in the dirt and trying to get his knees up so he could flip off his opponent and get on top, he had his father's height and shared his nose and eyes.

Jake Watkins, the mine foreman, was among those hollering encouragement to one fighter or the other, so Fargo stepped over and asked what was going on.

"Soon as his dad got back, little Charlie come up, wantin' to be of some use, so I sent him over to the sorting house, to muck the waste rock. Him and Pete Grover got into it, and they all know the rules."

"Rules?"

"If men here gotta fight, they do it at lunchtime, and they gotta fight reasonable fair. No weapons, no biting or clawing or any of that woman stuff."

Fargo nodded. "Sounds like as good a way as any to settle their arguments, I suppose. Why'd this start? Pete want to take the boss's bratty kid down a notch or two?"

Watkins examined the fight. Charlie had reversed Pete, and was now on top, working for a hammerlock on Pete's muscular right arm. Satisfied that it was still fair, he answered Fargo.

"Not really. Charlie's mighty green, an' he could have his run of the place, him bein' the owner's boy, but he really will pull his weight if'n you let him. Pete pretty much runs the sorting house, where we separate the good ore from the worthless country rock after it comes up on the skip. Way I heard it, Charlie wanted to wear gloves, and that started it all."

Gloves seemed reasonable if you had to handle either a shovel or rough, fresh-broken rock for any length of time. The mine foreman must have read the puzzled look on Fargo's face. "Pete says anybody that wears gloves is a pussy, an' he don't want 'em working around him. I know, it sounds silly to some, but us miners can be a curious and superstitious lot, Fargo. Most think the same way as Pete about gloves. Guess they figger that mashing a finger every now and again gives 'em something to brag on."

The fight was mostly scuffle and cuss at the moment. Jake hollered to Pete that eye-gouging wasn't allowed, even at Gouge-Eye's leading mine, and told

Charlie that he'd get his precious young hands stomped into jelly if he tried pulling Pete's hair again.

"Didn't figure on seeing the owner's son in a brawl like this," Fargo wondered.

"The old man left me strict orders that if the boy was going to hang around here with the men, he'd live by the same rules they do. It's my ass if he gets any special favors. So he don't."

Charlie, even though he lacked Pete's muscles, knew how to use his long body for leverage. Instead of staying right on top, he stretched perpendicular, his scuffed boots planted in the dirt. Shoving more with his knees than his arms, the boy pushed Pete's twisted arm past the limit of his resistance. Pete's head went deeper into the dirt. His legs kept kicking, but it was obvious that the older contestant wasn't going anywhere, no matter how much more he strained and sweated.

"Okay, men, it's over." The foreman consulted his pocket watch. "You fuckers got about fifteen minutes to chow down. Then it's assholes and elbows again." Watkins walked to the center of the dispersing ring. Young Charlie was on his feet. Watkins held up the boy's hand while Pete struggled to his feet. The miner glared hard, then swallowed some of his bile and shook the kid's hand as Watkins dropped it.

"Guess it's okay if you want to wear gloves from here on," Pete conceded as Charlie nodded and smiled.

The kid turned, saw Fargo, and gulped some, stepping back.

The Trailsman stood silent, getting a good look. Charlie Hamilton matched his height almost exactly. But the sandy-haired kid was just that, a kid, even if he had just soared through a growth spurt. Somewhat stoop-shouldered and hollow-chested, he was skinny, like a hanging piece of cord that might someday expand into a rope. He looked a lot like his dad, although where the old man grew a beard, he displayed a cloud of peach fuzz.

"Howdy, Charlie," Fargo said, stepping in on the kid.

Charlie's eyes darted as he sized up Fargo. "Who are you?"

"Skye Fargo."

"You the gent everybody's been talkin' about? The one that done stopped Pugnose's clock?" Fargo nodded, but that barely interrupted Charlie's chatter. "You just rode up and shot all them stage robbers, didn't you? And ain't you the one that walks the town with the gal that takes all her clothes off? Mister, I want to meet you."

"Well, you've done it." Fargo offered to shake. The awestruck kid kept staring at him, as if the Trailsman sported a dozen arms, each with a smoking six-shooter that had just plugged a notorious outlaw.

Finally Charlie grabbed his hand and started pumping it enthusiastically. "I just can't believe it. I've met Mr. Skye Fargo himself. How'd I do out there today, Mr. Fargo?"

"You fought just fine, Charlie. You didn't have Pete's muscles, but you had some leverage on him. So you avoided what he was good at, and used what you were good at. That's smart thinking. But that isn't why I came up to see you."

"You came up here just to see me?" The kid couldn't have showed any more excitement if he'd just gotten credit at a whorehouse.

Fargo nodded. "Indeed I did. Your pa's kind of worried about you. There anywhere we can jaw for a spell, more or less private?"

"There's the office. But you'd best clear that with Jake, er, Mr. Watkins."

Watkins overheard enough to nod their way, so they stepped into the office. Charlie waited for Fargo to settle into a rickety chair before settling atop an empty powder keg, his legs stretching halfway cross the tiny room.

"Why's my dad worried?" he piped, his voice shifting an octave or so between words.

"He says you need more schooling, and you won't learn much in Gouge-Eye except fighting, gambling, whoring, and the like."

Charlie slumped and his legs quit twitching quite so

much. "He said he was going to build a schoolhouse and bring in a teacher."

"He tried, Charlie, he tried. Your pa may be as decent as men get, and he may have a ton of money, but even he can't make Gouge-Eye into the kind of place where a teacher might stay. You think you need more schooling?"

Charlie blushed, and now his voice stammered and cracked while ranging up and down the scale. "Mr. Fargo, don't tell nobody, please. They already think I'm a sissy, no matter how much rock I can muck in a shift. But I kinda liked school. Not all of it, of course. Hated memorizing those stupid poems, and it plumb mortifies me to write anything. But I was just getting good at that algebra stuff, and then we come out here, and then Mom passed on, and, well, what I guess I'm trying to say is that I truly would like to learn more about numbers and how to work with 'em. And some more science stuff, too. I'd like to learn how they build them big bridges and locomotives and things like that."

Fargo nodded. "Nothing to be ashamed of in that, Charlie, nothing at all. So you wouldn't mind going back to school?"

"I s'pose not. But where's the school?"

Fargo knew that question was coming, and decided a straight answer was best. "In St. Louis."

"St. Louis? A boarding school? Where they have rules about when you get up and all that? They won't let you out to see the saloons and fancy gals?"

"Afraid so, Charlie. But I reckon you'll still be able to find saloons and fancy gals after you graduate."

Charlie mulled on that. "That's four or five years away, Mr. Fargo." His sullen expression made it clear that he considered that interval real close to eternity.

"It's my job to get you there if you want to go, Charlie. If you don't, just say the word, and I'll be on my way to somewhere else, and you can hang around here. You'll likely have a lot of fun watching the tinhorns fleece the miners every payday. You'll make friends with a few of the sporting gals, and maybe some of them won't have boyfriends that'll club you in the hallway and rifle your pockets. You'll develop a taste for the rotgut whiskey and pisswater beer they sell around here. You'll win a few more fistfights, probably lose a few too, and you'll get so damn good at moving a shovel that you'll get lots of respect from all the other stove-up three-fingered miners. You'll get to see a lot of gunfights, and if you're reasonably lucky, you'll not get shot in the process."

Charlie started to say something, but Fargo just went on. "And if you do want to learn your way around those numbers and formulas and whatnot, we'll ride east at sunup."

"Mr. Fargo, it's kind of scary, goin' away from home."

"It is."

Charlie's face showed evidence of hard thought. "But you'll be riding me clear to St. Louis? I'd get to cross the prairies with the Trailsman?"

"That's the plan, if you're agreeable."

Charlie smiled and nodded. "I guess that'd be all right, Mr. Fargo."

If Fargo stayed in Charlie's sight any longer, he was going to start feeling like an idol getting worshiped. Combine that with the swaggering reputation he'd already acquired here, and a man's hat could start feeling too small.

The Trailsman told the boy to get back to work. On his way down, he ran into Darius Hamilton and said they'd be leaving at sunrise tomorrow. The mine-owner couldn't have looked more pleased if his foreman had announced that they'd just struck a yard-wide vein of solid gold.

Fargo asked about equipment for the trip—a horse and saddle for Charlie, as well as a rig for Florence for as far as Webster, a couple of packsaddles and packhorses, and so forth.

"I keep my horse at the livery now, but there's a tack room behind the house. Get what you need there if you can find it—Lydia's old sidesaddle is there, I know." He paused and looked toward the town graveyard on the other side of the valley. "Horses? Not many around . . . No, wait. Ought to be some at the livery that used to belong to some men that're dead now. Somebody brought in the stage robbers' horses, I heard."

Fargo nodded and started preparing for the trip. One preparation he really wanted to make involved Florence. But she insisted on staying in Hamilton's guest room that night, by herself.

5

Florence Trefethen had caught the eastbound stage at Webster two days ago, and Fargo was beginning to suspect she'd had the right idea. Mile by mile, a man on horseback could easily stay ahead of the lumbering, swaying Concord coaches. But day by day, the coach generally came out ahead.

For the stage, there were fresh horses waiting every fifteen or twenty miles, so the driver could push his animals hard. Plus, the meals were waiting for the passengers, so all they had to do was eat and move on. If they stopped for the night, it was a short night, and nobody that was involved with moving on had to worry about camp chores. The would-be schoolmarm aboard the Denver and South Park Stage Line should be to Denver by now.

Skye Fargo and Charlie Hamilton couldn't push their mounts. They couldn't swap to fresh horses, and they had to stop and tend their critters when the stage could have kept rolling on. They had to hustle their own grub, and other camp chores took considerable time. They were still up in the mountains, jammed in a twisting steep-walled canyon that really didn't have enough room for both the roaring creek and the wagon road that generally hugged its south bank.

This day had started bright and so clear that the soaring peaks looked close enough to grab. Out of habit, Fargo scanned the looming ridges. Not much to worry about up there, being as the only Indians hereabouts were the Utes, and they'd been behaving themselves lately.

But above those sawtooth ridges, the sky wasn't blue anymore. It was somber and gloomy. The darkness had come quickly, as if some giant had snapped a wool blanket across the heavens. This wasn't a nice summer day anymore.

The kid rode ahead on a dappled gelding that had belonged to a stage robber. He trailed the mount Florence had ridden to Webster, a placid roan mare now toting a packsaddle.

"Charlie," Fargo advised, "you keep your eyes peeled for a spot to hole up for a couple hours."

Charlie scanned such sky as they could see between the gray granite canyon walls—the firmament was pretty much the same color now as the rock—then responded. "If'n it rains, I've got a brand-new vulcanized rubber slicker."

"Ain't a damn one of them that keeps you comfortable through much more than a sprinkle." Fargo pulled up to ride abreast with the kid. "Besides, you sweat so much inside a slicker that you get about as wet as if you hadn't bothered."

"Then why carry slickers at all?"

"Because they're better than nothing." The first cold raindrops pelted at the Trailsman's face as he drew back, hoping there would be a shack around the next bend.

There wasn't. Being sure about that took some hard staring, because the rain was coming harder and the boiling black clouds seemed to be descending on them. But they had time for a good look, because they stopped and pulled on their rain gear. "Shouldn't we get up high as we can, Mr. Fargo? I saw a flash flood once rip down a canyon."

"Seen that myself a time or two," Fargo replied as icy rain leaked down his neck to join the pool of hot sweat already forming in the small of his back. "Shelter would suit me fine. I reckon we could settle for whatever comes first, a roof or a side gulch we can ride up."

Charlie nodded and they resumed their course through the darkening afternoon, bend after bend lined by near-vertical ramparts.

Then their constricted world lit up with an instant of blue flash, brighter than the sun. A tremendous bolt seemed to jump from just in front of them, clawing its way skyward to meet another blue-white fireball that punched downward from the coal-black core of the cloud that enveloped them.

For an eye blink, the visible world froze. The horses had plodding hooves suspended in midgait. Spray and splatter hung above the rocks in the creek. Charlie sat straight up, staring at the blinding thunderbolt not a hundred yards before him. It couldn't have been much farther than that, because the deafening crack of thunder came even before the image faded.

The dappled gelding had never before come so close to having its eardrums shattered. The critter decided to protest. Amid the pounding echoes off the canyon walls, it reared. Its front hooves thrashed toward the source of the explosion as the horse tried to stand straight on its two hind legs. Charlie jerked the reins. His horse started down, then crow-hopped.

Almost out of his saddle, the sliding kid grabbed for the horn as Fargo prodded his Ovaro forward. He couldn't blame his own mount for being reluctant, what with both a headstrong critter and the very recent memory of that flash and noise up there, but this wasn't the time for the Ovaro to argue. He pushed through the driving rain, hoping to grab Charlie off the horse.

The kid's long legs kept him aboard for the second or two it took Fargo to get there. Not daring to drop the Ovaro's reins in this horse-spooking weather, Fargo held them in his left hand and swung his right around, trying to grab Charlie's shoulders.

The gelding had other ideas, now that it had decided everything around was up to no good. Still bucking, the dappled animal shied away from the Ovaro, twisting toward the creek. Charlie got thrown over the side before Fargo could grab him. The gelding took off, dragging the confused pack mare.

Expecting to have to pick up Charlie after a hard fall, Fargo instantly swung down and stepped toward the creek, standing where the agitated horses had just been.

No Charlie. Nothing but goddamn rocks and water.

The Trailsman snapped his head up and looked down the road, his view improved by a lightning flash, this one less awful because it was at least a quarter-mile away. There were the bouncing rumps of two spooked horses galloping around the bend. The front one was dragging something, off to one side. Charlie had managed to keep one foot in a stirrup, even if the rest of him wasn't on the horse. He was getting dragged along this rocky road, a process that could quickly turn a man into a heap of bloody mush.

Cursing himself for not realizing sooner what had happened, even if there hadn't been a way to see it, Fargo jumped aboard his big pinto. Catching up didn't take long, even if it involved crossing the creek at the ford just past the next bend. The gelding and the roan were trying to hurry, but Charlie's lanky body slowed them down.

Fargo tried not to think about that. But the gelding gave Fargo plenty to worry about, even after he got abreast of it. The wide-eyed frightened horse was still jumping and lunging. Hooking himself into his saddle, Fargo leaned low to grab at its drooping reins.

He came up with the close one, which snapped off in his hand as soon as he tried to yank it. Hoping the Ovaro had enough sense not to stumble here, Fargo straightened and kneed his mount against the panicked gelding.

The Trailsman's long arms got around the horse's slick neck. Fargo pushed himself out of the Ovaro's saddle and rolled aboard the gelding. He jammed his knees into its flanks, then whipped off his broad-brimmed hat and leaned forward. With one arm, he pressed the rain-softened felt against the gelding's eyes, because the only way this horse was going to see reason was to quit seeing at all. With his free hand, he made sure by grabbing the bridle's cheek bar and pulling up.

Between instant blindness and getting its breath choked, the dappled gelding settled down in seconds. The trick now was to get Charlie's foot free. That meant dismounting, which would give the horse time to run off again before Fargo could get the twisted foot out of the stirrup. But it didn't make much sense to just sit out there in the ice-cold pelting rain, waiting for someone to happen along who could help out.

The sky was still popping all around them, and with every flash of lighting or roll of thunder, the gelding tensed and wanted to light out again. Fargo had to keep himself draped on the horse's neck, one hand holding the blindfold hat while the other twisted the bit.

Killing the horse while it quivered under him seemed the most reasonable course. But this wasn't really the horse's fault—any animal, no matter how generally even-tempered, got frightened sometimes, and a thunderbolt striking that close was plenty of excuse. Dragging Charlie hadn't been the horse's idea. So the notion of shooting it was damn near as disgusting as what Fargo knew he would see whenever he could get down to Charlie.

Try something else first. Fargo twisted and the saddle horn dug into his gut. He slid his right foot down, finally reaching the stirrup with his foot.

It would have been easier if he could see what he was doing, but then life would have been easier if he didn't have to do this at all. His own nudging boot felt Charlie's. The way it hung in the stirrup, Charlie's whole foot must have slipped forward, clear through the opening, just before he pitched off. Down on the ground and getting dragged, there was no way he could get enough slack to twist his boot to an angle that the heel would clear. And his boots must have fit him well, so well they wouldn't come off without a bootjack assisted by wriggling and pulling.

Prodding gingerly with his right foot while he immobilized the horse, Fargo hooked his toe under the stirrup and rocked it. There was some slack, some room to work. The nudging got tedious, especially when the rain poured like a cow pissing on a flat rock.

But the gelding seemed to understand that it would be dead if it moved. That was one less thing to worry about as Fargo finally got Charlie's boot heel up and through the stirrup. Moments later, the still leg splashed down to join the rest of the boy in the rocks and mud.

Not really caring what the gelding did now, Fargo eased himself off and knelt next to the battered form. Charlie's slicker was in tatters, as was his shirt. His chest and shoulders looked like somebody had taken a hammer to him, but they looked better than his head. Charlie was bleeding from a scalp cut, one ear, his nose, and maybe a couple other spots. He lay there gape-mouthed, his eyes glazed, looking up, his lips a pale purple.

The way the rain was hitting, Fargo couldn't really tell if the kid's chest was still moving. He knelt lower and felt relief as his whiskers moved in response to Charlie's shallow breathing. The kid was alive. Just how alive, and for how long, were good questions. The boy's clammy skin felt cold, so the likely answer wasn't promising.

Fargo studied his options, and nothing sounded good. He had to get Charlie somewhere warm and comfortable if the boy was going to pull through. Where they were, with him lying on the rocks while the chilling rain poured over his battered body, was about as far from warm and comfortable as places ever got. Moving him, though, was risky. He sure as hell couldn't sit up, much less ride, and there weren't any wagons handy. Besides, if he'd busted any bones along the way, even lifting him might hurt more than it would help.

Fargo cussed some at the weather, to no apparent effect. He aimed a few oaths at the skittish gelding that now stood nearby, quiet as a plow horse after spring planting.

After spreading his own slicker over Charlie's sprawled form, more out of manners than any belief that it would help, Fargo pulled his bedroll off the packsaddle. Coated with a mixture of coal oil and beeswax, its canvas cover shed water pretty well. Maybe well enough to keep the wool blankets inside reasonably dry, even when the rain came this fiercely. And even when it got wet, wool would keep a man warm.

Naturally, by the time Fargo wrestled the inert Charlie, along with a bunch of mud and goop, into the blankets, the rain started to ease up. Mountain thunderstorms were like that, coming and going without much in the way of introductions or farewells. In what seemed like moments to the busy Trailsman, the sky got blue, the sun began to light and heat the world again, and Charlie showed more signs of life by starting to shiver at a furious pace.

Even in the summer, soaked people could more or less freeze to death. Fargo didn't know the exact way it happened, although a sawbones had once explained that when folks got chilled enough on the outside, they could get cold inside too. Once their vital organs got too cold, they quit working right, although it could take a while before everything stopped and they died.

Fargo knew his only hope was to get the kid somewhere warm and dry. While wrestling the kid into the bedroll, he hadn't noticed any broken bones, unless maybe in that ankle that had been stuck in the stirrup. Perhaps he could move the boy safely if there was a way to haul him.

The Indians had a way, and Fargo used it. He fetched a hatchet from his gear and cut down two reasonably straight aspen saplings, each about twenty feet long. The Trailsman trimmed them, then lashed them together in a V shape, weaving the rope between the legs. He rolled Charlie atop the travois. With his last length of rope, he lashed the bedroll to where it would stay put.

He moved as much as he could off the pack frame and onto the gelding's saddle. The roan mare seemed calm enough to handle the travois; his Ovaro didn't much like pulling things, and if there was a choice, Fargo avoided it. Finally rigged, they started moving as the sun sank lower behind them.

There had to be a stage station not too far down the road, Fargo knew. Even as slow as they had to go, to keep from bouncing the heavy travois any more than necessary, it couldn't take more than three or four hours. But then he remembered the trip up, less than a fortnight ago. Jackpine Junction wasn't even a junction, just a place to change horses. There was a shack for the horse tender, a foul-smelling gent who wasn't likely to have a tub for the hot bath Charlie sure needed. Nor was the man likely to offer much more hospitality than Fargo could provoke with his Colt.

If that's what had to be done, he'd do it. The shadows were already getting long when Fargo saw a side road. He searched his memory. Skull Gulch. A placer camp only a mile or two up off the stage road.

To be more accurate, Skull Gulch had been a placer camp, for about two months the summer before last. A few nuggets had been found in the creek and men rushed in, throwing up maybe a dozen log cabins. But there weren't many nuggets. After the first week, such pay dirt as anybody found was powdery flour gold, tiny specks that were more trouble than they were worth. The town was deserted even before the aspen started their fall color change.

But the narrow road that climbed to his right said something different than what Fargo knew of Skull Gulch, because it hadn't started to grow over. It had seen considerable traffic recently. And even if that activity was meant for some new strike above Skull Gulch, there had to be something left to the abandoned town, some kind of shelter with a fireplace or a stove, some way he could get Charlie warm sooner than he could at Jackpine Junction.

The well-used road wasn't the only curious thing about Skull Gulch. The cabins were obviously occupied, showing evidence of recent chinking and new shingles, and there was smoke wafting from chimneys and stovepipes. Some of the placer diggings along the creek looked fresh enough. But not a human being could be seen when Fargo rode in.

"Hello, the house," Fargo shouted at the first building he rode up to. He kept his hand on his Colt, but he didn't get any answer of any kind. He knew damn well somebody was nearby, because smoke was drifting out the stovepipe, and he could smell dinner cooking inside. He moved to the next cabin. It showed similar evidence that somebody was inside, but again, nothing happened when he called out. This was getting spooky. He'd heard of ghost towns, but this was the first one where the ghosts appeared to have any need to cook dinner.

At the fourth house, Fargo finally got a reply. A window shutter opened just enough to allow a rifle barrel to stick out. "What you want, mister?"

"My friend here got dragged by a horse today," the Trailsman explained, trying to sound more friendly than he felt. "He got beat up pretty bad, and he's cold, too. I'm trying to find a place where he can rest up for a spell."

"Who you are?" The words were coming out in a strange order, but there really wasn't an accent, not enough of one, anyway, for Fargo to place.

"Skye Fargo. My friend in the travois is Charlie Hamilton, from up at Gouge-Eye."

"You no mean hurt us?" The rifle dropped and Fargo released his grip on his Colt.

"I'm not fixing to hurt anybody," he replied, "unless somebody keeps me from tending to my friend."

"Come on foot to door."

Fargo hadn't planned on riding into their front room anyway, so he dismounted and untied the lead rope from the roan, then attached it to a hitching rail. Before going to the door, he checked on Charlie, who was still unconscious, blue-lipped, shivering and shaking like a dog coming out of the water.

The man who answered the door was damn near as wide as the frame, although he barely came up to Fargo's shoulders. Below his black queue, he had on a loose pullover shirt and wore baggy cotton trousers. "I am Hop Sing, Mr. Fargo. Please do in come."

Fargo stepped inside and shook hands. "Pleased to make your acquaintance, Mr. Hop."

The man brightened. "You have been among our people before, I see. You know our way with names."

Fargo nodded, glad that he had remembered that Chinese folk put their last name first and first name last. Then he told his stomach to quit growling so loud over the spicy aromas coming from another room in the cabin. Even the sounds of cutlery and cookware reminded him of his hunger.

"Mr. Fargo, please our rudeness forgive. White strangers usually bring us no good."

That was the damn truth. Chinamen got stoned,

mobbed, and tortured all over the West. Most miners despised them. Fargo had never quite figured out why. The Chinese worked hard and well. Maybe too well and hard, because the miners claimed they would do too much work for too little pay, thus keeping the white workers from drawing better wages. The Chinese did tend to be clannish, which was understandable, given the hostility they faced any time they weren't among themselves. Since they would toil so persistently, they could eke out livings in places the other miners had given up on—like Skull Gulch.

"My friend out there," Fargo said. "He needs to come inside a lot more than I do."

Hop Sing grabbed his wide conical straw hat, stepped into some sandals, and walked outside with Fargo. After looking at Charlie, he clapped his hands loudly and shouted something melodious that Fargo couldn't understand. The other folks in Skull Gulch understood, though, because they came running out.

A rail-thin elderly gent with a drooping white mustache took the longest look at shivering Charlie. He must have been the settlement's doctor or medicine man or whatever. "He need hot bath," he told Fargo. "He bruised bad. Hurt awful when come to. I have herbs and potions for making him well. Bring him my house. I tend."

That sounded like the best offer they were going to get, so Fargo led the roan down the street about a hundred yards, to the far edge of town. Using the makeshift travois as a litter, half a dozen townsmen helped Fargo tote Charlie inside. The doctor's front room belied the cabin's rough exterior. Silk tapestries covered the walls, the floor had a thick carpet, and the place reeked of sweet-smelling incense that smoldered in dragon-shaped brass burners. Fargo was just as glad to get back outside.

Hop Sing seemed to be the headman here. Whenever he said something, people scurried off. "You will eat with us, Mr. Fargo, while your friend gets well. Wan Lo says he mend quick, less than week." They got to Hop Sing's cabin. "My house is small, Mr. Fargo, or you stay here. You use house back there?"

It was more of a shed than a house, but it looked tight, and Fargo didn't see any reason to be too picky. It held a cot and a little stove, without space for much else, but it was cleaner than a lot of hotel rooms he'd paid good money for. After Fargo said the room would be fine with him and explained that Charlie was using his bedroll, Hop Sing sent one of his kids out with some sheets and blankets.

As soon as the little boy got back and Fargo could quit pretending that he liked the bitter green tea that came in a tiny ceramic cup that was too small to suit his big hands, they had dinner around an oilcloth-covered kitchen table.

Nothing familiar like a fork or spoon was at hand. Fargo tried pinching the food with his chopsticks, but the stuff kept sliding out before he could get it to his mouth. He watched Hop Sing and his two sons, both boys of seven or eight. They used their chopsticks like a spoon, sliding them under the food, so Fargo did the same.

Dinner was beef, sliced into paper-thin strips and coated with batter, then fried in hot oil with some local greens and chopped roots. Although there were Chinese cooks most everywhere Fargo had traveled, they stuck to American steak, stew, beans, and potatoes, never producing their native delicacies. Maybe delicacy wasn't the right word. Mrs. Hop, a tiny round woman who hovered near the stove throughout the meal, could have taught the Mexicans some new tricks about mixing fire with food. No chili in Fargo's considerable experience even came close.

Every bite seemed intent on burning a hole in the Trailsman's tongue, lips, palate, and throat. He tried to be polite about it and sit reasonably still between gulps of tea, instead of following his sensible impulse to grab the five-gallon water bucket in the kitchen and drain it. Hop Sing just sat there, working his chopsticks, as did his two young sons.

Fargo got the feeling this was some kind of test, to see just how much of a man he was by how much fire his belly could take. He figured he passed when they all got up and Hop Sing smiled and asked if he needed to borrow a lantern to find his room. Panting and gulping and gritting his teeth between words, the Trailsman said he'd manage on his own. He knew for damn sure he could find that creek full of cold water, and that's the only place he really had to go.

6

The Trailsman shifted his big frame, trying to find some way to get more comfortable atop the cot that was about six inches shorter than he was. He gave up on the effort—nothing had worked on the preceding three nights, either—and relaxed. No matter how short the cot, though, a day of hard work made a man ready to drop right off to sleep, and he'd managed that.

Charlie appeared to be on the mend. Fargo dropped by morning and evening to check on the kid. After a hot bath the first night, and then Wan Lo's balms and tonics, the boy was sitting up, even standing some. He didn't seem to be hurting much, although he still seemed a bit addleheaded every time Fargo visited, talking more slowly than usual, with a dreamy, far-off look on his bruised face. But he'd be ready to ride on soon.

Hating to wait idly, even though the Chinese insisted that he was their guest and so he didn't have to do much more than lift his chopsticks at mealtime, Fargo worked the placers with his hosts. After tending to his gear the first day, he'd helped lever some table-sized boulders out of the way, so the men could get to whatever gold might lie underneath. The past two days had been spent working a whipsaw with Hop Sing, cutting felled trees into planks for new sluice boxes, rockers, and long toms.

Perhaps two dozen people inhabited Skull Gulch. All were Chinese. Only Hop Sing appeared to have a family here. He'd explained that their group—they were all related, more or less—had left China about ten years ago after an agent promised them jobs in America. Although some of the other men were married, they'd left their wives behind, planning either to send for them when they had a stake, or to return to their homeland with all the money they'd made in the United States.

In total darkness, Fargo stretched, sending his feet out from under the blankets to hang over the end of the cot. Then he lay back, knowing sleep would arrive in moments. It would have, except he heard some scratching at the door. More annoyed than alarmed, he reached for his revolver. "Somebody out there?" he inquired as he sat up.

The reply was a whisper. "Yes. It is I, Sun Li. May I enter?"

Sun Li, whoever he was, didn't sound dangerous. "Sure. The latch string's out."

The door moved slowly, almost silently. Fargo couldn't see Sun Li worth mention. The visitor couldn't be very big, though, or the floor would be creaking some under his steps. Arriving with Sun Li was a sweet aroma, no doubt that of incense that lingered in clothes and hair. The door closed behind Sun Li.

"Can I do something for you, Sun Li?" Fargo swung around and set his feet on the floor.

"Most sincerely Sun Li hope so." The voice was still a whisper, but higher-pitched than at first. "You need not rise for me, please." The visitor sat down on the bed next to Fargo, and he felt a small hand sliding across his shoulder.

"You're a gal," was all the flustered Trailsman could say while her hand moved down his chest.

"Sun Li most curious, Fargo Skye."

He turned toward her as her hand reached his waist and began to move under the covers. "Well, Miss Sun, I'll do my best to answer your questions."

Her other tiny hand reached Fargo's torso, and he did a little exploring on his own. She was tiny, dressed in a loose Mother Hubbard. Fargo quickly discovered she didn't have much, if anything, on beneath it. He felt her pointed nipples rise, atop firm breasts that were in perfect proportion to the rest of her. She seemed intent on leaning forward and kissing, so Fargo obliged, pulling her against him.

After her flickering tongue probed his mouth, Sun

Li came up for air. "Fargo Skye, Sun Li must know if what she has heard is true."

What did this petite woman have in mind? Was she trying to learn something, or was she planning to have some fun? Since Fargo couldn't see her, he couldn't read her face. But from the way she responded when he lay back and pulled her with him, and then worked his hand up a silken and eager thigh beneath the loose gown, he was pretty sure she had pleasure in mind.

Her hands were busy, too—so busy that Fargo had to proceed slowly to get her out of her Mother Hubbard gown. While her legs dangled over the edge of the cot, her feet off the floor, he managed to tug the garment away from her smooth thighs and writhing buttocks, past the tiny waist, past her pert breasts, which made him linger for a minute or two. Then he had to get her to lift her arm, but Sun Li didn't want to let go, even for the instant it would take to push the robe off.

She had her little hands tight on his tool, grasping and squeezing the shaft while her thumbs stroked the tip, slowly and tantalizingly. Fargo didn't really want her to let go, either. It was a bit awkward, wrestling the bunched-up gown over her head. He relieved her of it, but the process was slow, one arm at a time while she continued to hold and stroke him.

"It must be so," was all Sun Li said through the whole process. Fargo enjoyed her handwork, but he figured it was time to move on. After tossing the gown to the floor, he lay back, pulling Sun Li with him, and their lips met again. Her hands were now up on his shoulders, but she wasn't neglecting his throbbing erection.

She was too short to reach it, but she had it grasped between her smooth knees. Sun Li slid them forward and back, slowly and only an inch or two with each silken undulation. Her pliant breasts pressed against him, at the top of his torso, just under his neck, the nipples feeling almost sharp and hard enough to leave marks.

Knowing he'd never wanted anything more than he wanted Sun Li right now, Fargo moved his hands along her narrow back, his palms at her sides while his fingertips met along her writhing spine. He felt the swell of her buttocks and pressed, urging her moist and ready body downward.

Sun Li responded, but in her own good time. She opened her knees. Her thighs gripped his hips while she planted fervent kisses against his neck. She wriggled her open cleft against the Trailsman's abdomen, spreading her musky dampness and impressing it upon him. His belly tightened under the smooth slickness of her open slit, and her scant pubic hair almost tickled.

Fargo didn't want to waste a load into the night air, but he knew he couldn't wait much longer. He tried to think about something else while Sun Li's hips slinked toward his navel. All he could think about was that it had been a while since he'd been with a woman, too damn long, and that cussed schoolmarm up in Gouge-Eye hadn't helped a bit.

"Now," he urged, "let's go." He grasped Sun Li's hips and arched his pelvis. The way she was weaving, it was just as well his pulsating shaft knew how to find its own way home. Her wet flesh clamped the tip as soon as it probed inward.

The Trailsman thrust higher, harder. It was time. It was past time. She rolled upward, impaling herself as she settled to engulf him with great astonished gasps. After taking him in deep, she bent forward again and resumed her back-and-forth sliding while her internal muscles amplified the pleasure.

Fargo erupted. So did Sun Li, in a furious tumult that had her body rocking up against his, then swinging back to where he could feel her hair brush his knees, then forward again to impel her agitated breasts against his heaving rib cage.

From the sound and feel of it, Fargo reckoned she'd had enough. But he guessed wrong. When he started to disengage and turn to his side, she slid her legs back and rolled right with him, keeping him inside her as she lay with her back to the wall. Fargo didn't know how she did it; her tight interior seemed as dexterous as her hands at applying subtle but provocative pressures. But he sure wasn't going to complain, although he felt pretty lethargic after the third go-round, with him on top and her little feet pressed up against his ears.

All that time, she hadn't said anything Fargo could comprehend, although Sun Li occasionally uttered hushed remarks in Chinese. Finally, she pulled herself away from his side. "Sun Li must go now," she announced.

Since she lived here and he didn't, Fargo figured she had good reasons for lighting out in the middle of the night. The Chinese had treated him fine, but their notions of hospitality doubtlessly didn't extend quite this far.

"Just a minute," he said as she stood next to the cot and pulled her Mother Hubbard down. "Didn't you say you had a question? Something you wanted to know?"

"Sun Li know now. You already give me answer," she whispered back. "The stories were true."

"What stories?"

"They say white men all big, big like horse. Stay hard long time. Can pleasure woman all night. So, when Fargo Skye come to Skull Gulch, Sun Li decide to find out if that all true. Sun Li try learn more next night if Fargo Skye still here."

The Trailsman didn't quite know what to say to that, so he just muttered good-bye as she slipped out the door. The grass always looked greener on the other side of the fence, and some folks just couldn't help but be curious. And answering her questions was a damn sight more pleasant than answering Charlie's, Fargo decided before nodding off.

Steaming green tea wasn't Fargo's favorite morning eye-opener, but he sure needed something to clear out his grogginess. He couldn't have slept more than two or three hours, and these Chinese seemed to think it was downright sinful not to be hard at work by dawn. Fargo didn't want to let on that anything unusual had happened last night, since that might get Sun Li in trouble with the rest of the tong. If the Chinese were anything like most other tight groups, they could get

mean when one of their women got too close to somebody that looked different.

But was she somebody's woman? During daylight,
Fargo had never seen any females around Skull Gulch,
except for Mrs. Hop. She'd either cooled down her
cooking, or else he was developing a tolerance for the
throat-charring spices. So when he got over to Wan
Lo's that morning, he asked the thin, white-haired
healer if there were any womenfolk in town besides
Mrs. Hop.

"So you have the urge?" The doctor gave Fargo a
sly man-to-man smile.

"Is there a man that doesn't? But that's not why I
asked. Just thought I saw a gal the other day, out
of the corner of my eye, but I wasn't sure." Fargo
remained standing, brushing off Wan Lo's gesture
toward a big pillow on the carpet. The place made
Fargo uncomfortable, and he didn't want to stay any
longer than necessary.

"You saw Sun Li. Poor girl. Her honorable mother
and father died of fever on the trail last year when we
came to Colorado from California. She stay with us,
takes in our washing. She knows not what to do,
without parents to arrange her marriage. The rest of
her family remains in the Celestial Empire." Wan Lo
accompanied him through the bead curtain into the
small side room where Charlie was recovering.

Clad in some silk pajamas that were so short that
the sleeves didn't get much past his elbows, the boy
put down a book and sat up straighter to greet them.
"Hi, Mr. Fargo."

" 'Morning, Charlie. How you feeling?"

"Just fine. Doc Wan here says I'll be ready to ride
on in a couple days, good as new."

Fargo turned to Wan Lo and saw confirmation in
the man's squinting eyes.

"Sounds good, Charlie. It's plumb amazing, how
fast you're coming around after the pounding you
took."

"Well, nothing serious got busted. My ankle was
twisted bad and swole up fit to explode, but that

stinkful salve the doc puts on it has it back to near normal now."

"You need anything, Charlie?"

"Oh, no, Mr. Fargo."

"You're not getting bored, just lying around?"

"I sleep plenty. Dream a lot. And Doc Wan showed me how to work his abacus." He pointed to the framework of wires and beads next to the cup of water and some other clutter next to his mat. "He even lent me this here algebra book. I'm gettin' a handle on them quadratic equations now. Want to see?"

Fargo shook his head. "No, that's all just so much hen-scratching to me, Charlie. But I'm glad you're working at your ciphering."

Out in the parlor, with its gaudy tapestries and clouds of incense, Fargo asked Wan Lo for more details about Charlie's recovery.

"The boy's doing fine, Mr. Fargo."

"How long before we can head on?"

"As he said, a day or two. More rest would not hurt, of course. He was bruised quite badly. Those are healing quickly. But they will be most tender and painful until the healing is completed. It would be for the best if he did not risk having those places injured again."

It was summer, just the middle of July. They didn't have to rush to get to St. Louis in time for school to start. Staying here two or three more days wouldn't matter all that much, and if that meant Charlie would be in better shape for eight hundred miles of riding, Fargo would consider the time well spent. Besides, Sun Li might need answers to a few more questions. If he were going to keep Charlie on the straight and narrow along the trail, there wouldn't be many other opportunities to enjoy a woman's company. He stepped to the door, then turned.

"Dr. Wan, how much do we owe you?"

"It was my honor to be of assistance to a traveler in need, Mr. Fargo."

"I'm sure it was. But honor buys precious few groceries, Doc. Doubt it'll buy you even a stick of incense."

He smiled. "Confucius did not say that, but perhaps

the venerable sage should have. Whatever you can spare will be most appreciated, Mr. Fargo."

Fargo stifled a yawn and handed Wan Lo a pair of double-eagles. Maybe he could have spared more, but the doctor looked pleased enough. Then he found Hop Sing, who was too polite to comment on the way that Fargo, usually an energetic worker, was dragging ass all day while they sliced tree trunks into planks.

Perhaps Sun Li was a little disappointed by that night's lesson in the bedroom ways of exotic foreign men, because Fargo managed only two go-rounds with her. But if she was, she didn't let on. In fact, she sounded mighty contented. And Fargo made it up to her the next two nights.

He sure hoped Charlie was getting enough rest for the both of them, though. Between fourteen-hour days working either a saw or a shovel, and those sessions with Sun Li every night, Fargo sure wasn't getting rest worth mention.

Since Charlie was up and walking around one morning, Fargo decided that was as good a time as any to move on. Dr. Wan wasn't around that day, though, since he'd gone up in the hills to gather herbs. But the rest of the tong stood along the street to wave good-bye and thank Fargo for working with them. Even Sun Li came out of her little cabin where she did laundry.

It wasn't until they were setting up camp that evening, just outside Jackpine Junction, that anything seemed to be peculiar about Charlie. He'd been riding well, albeit not as talkative as usual. But then he hauled in an armload of firewood and sagged to the ground, scratching himself all over like he had hungry fire ants crawling over him.

"What's the matter, Charlie?"

"Startin' to hurt all over my body, Mr. Fargo. Time for my medicine, I guess."

"What medicine?"

"Didn't Doc Wan give you some medicine to bring along? To give me when the pain come up?"

"He was out this morning, remember? I didn't see him. But he said you'd be ready to ride out today."

"Oh, shit." Charlie doubled up, looking like he'd

just been kicked in the belly. Then he rubbed and clawed at himself some more.

Fargo knelt and grabbed the twitching boy's shoulders. "What kind of medicine did he have in mind? Maybe we can figure out something." Fargo shook Charlie, to look into his agonized, twisted face. "Think, Charlie. It won't be easy. I can see you're hurting. But I can't do a damn thing for you unless you explain to me."

Charlie took a labored breath. "Whenever I started to hurt fearful, he gave me some stuff called 'afyon.' "

"Doesn't mean anything to me. What'd it look like? Was this afyon you swallowed a pill or a powder or what?"

"Didn't swallow it, Mr. Fargo." Charlie gulped and shook some more. "Smoked it out of a pipe. Was little black balls, like rat turds."

The precise nature of afyon was starting to dawn on Fargo, but he wanted to be sure. "And what happened after you smoked it?"

"I quit hurtin', that's what. Felt all warm and good inside." He twisted, almost breaking loose of Fargo's grasp. "Made me feel all dreamy. I gotta have some. Feels like there's a big-toothed timber saw cuttin' my belly in half now."

Fargo released Charlie to curl up and writhe on the grass. The Trailsman stood. "Goddamnit, Charlie, do you know what that afyon stuff was?"

"No, sir," he muttered while rolling over.

"Jesus Christ," Fargo swore. "It was opium." Fargo stepped back, to keep from accidentally kicking Charlie in his growing rage, mostly directed at himself. Here he'd hired on to get the kid safely to St. Louis without picking up a taste for whiskey, cigars, cards, dice, or fancy gals. And that son of a bitch Wan Lo gives the boy a goddamn opium habit. Fargo kicked the closest rock.

"Opium," Charlie muttered, grasping his arms against his belly.

Fargo felt like riding back up to Skull Gulch and taking a horsewhip to Wan Lo, but Charlie needed his attention at the moment. The Trailsman kicked three more unyielding rocks and stomped some, just to get most of the anger out of his system. Then he knelt again next to Charlie.

"Well, kid, you are gonna hurt, and hurt like you were roasting in the lowest pit of hell for the next couple hours. But I'll be goddamned if you take that fucking opium habit any farther than right here."

Charlie started chewing hard on his lower lip at this announcement. "I'm sorry, Mr. Fargo," he stuttered between bites.

Fargo shook his head. "Not your fault, I reckon. You were just minding your elders, like a good kid. My fault, my fault entirely. I should have paid more mind to how Wan Lo was tending you." He silently added that Sun Li had been a considerable distraction, too, to make him neglect his responsibilities.

Charlie started to quiver and looked colder than he had after getting dragged through a thunderstorm. Fargo stayed close while he got the fire going. He fetched more wood. This promised to be a long and miserable night.

It was. The boy was racked with spasm after spasm of pain. Some of it was real, no doubt, from all his bumps and aches, pains that he just hadn't felt before because whenever they started, Wan Lo would show up with the pipe. Charlie would drift off into a dreamland where he felt no pain. And some of his agony came because a body could develop a craving for opium the same way some men's systems demanded whiskey or tobacco.

But along about midnight, when the Big Dipper swung farthest to the east, Charlie finally fell into a troubled, restless sleep. An hour or so later, his breathing got more regular and he even began to snore a bit. Fargo judged that the worst was over, and got such rest as he could.

Next morning, Charlie said his joints felt like they'd been hammered on, and his nose was running so much he filled up two bandannas before they got saddled up and moving. But he was clearheaded, and back to normal. He was chattering like a magpie, curious about what had just happened to him.

Fargo explained as best he knew.

"Is Dr. Wan Lo a bad man, Mr. Fargo?"

Fargo studied on that for a minute. It would be easy to say that Wan Lo was some sort of degenerate asshole that went around enslaving innocent youths. And if word of this ever got out, the whiskey-sotted, tobacco-chewing miners of the area would form an ugly mob and invade Skull Gulch, to wreak something awful on some hardworking people who'd treated Skye Fargo and Charlie Hamilton, in a time of need, as best they knew how.

"No, Charlie, Wan Lo isn't really a bad man, even if I'm mad as hell at the gent."

Past Jackpine Junction, the road swung away from the creek, because the canyon was just too damn narrow. They crested a rise. Instead of the usual view of a rolling valley and another rise, the Great Plains appeared before them, stretching eastward, clear to the edge of the world. Fargo let the horses blow a bit.

"Why do you say he's not a bad man if he did such a bad thing, giving me opium like that?"

"Charlie, I don't know if I have a good answer." He nudged the Ovaro with his knees, glad that he could finally see his way out of these damn mountains. "But they have their ways, and we have ours. There are a lot of good things about their ways. You saw how clean that camp was, and how there weren't a bunch of drunks shooting at one another when they weren't cheating at cards. I don't know a lot of their history, but I know their ancestors invented paper and printing and gunpowder a long time before our people did."

"Didn't they build a huge wall that went for miles and miles? Big enough to drive a stage on its top?"

"I read something about that once," Fargo responded. "But what I was getting at is that their ways are different from ours. They don't think there's a damn thing wrong with that opium stuff. And maybe in a Chinese town, there isn't. But you aren't Chinese. You won't be living in their places. And our people just don't have a lot of use for the stuff, or for men who walk around dreamy-eyed all the time, not too sure what's real and what isn't. Besides that, you can get an awful craving for it. You know a lot better than I do what it's like when you get used to smoking it and then there isn't any to be found."

Charlie nodded. "That's for sure, Mr. Fargo. Last night was pure torment till I fell asleep. And today I ache something awful in places that I didn't even know I had."

The road, after wending over the foothills crosswise, finally found a convenient draw and got serious about dropping on out to the plains. Two long, dust-churning mule-drawn trains of freight passed, headed uphill. About an hour later, Fargo recognized the familiar dust-covered green of a Concord stagecoach. But it wasn't moving. The driver stood at its front, bent over and disconnecting the harness tugs from the whiffle-tree, which had snapped right in the middle.

"Goddamn shit-for-brains jackleg wainwrights this miserable cheapskate outfit hires oughtta know better'n to use pissant knot-filled yellow pine for a job that takes stout white oak."

Fargo stepped over and allowed that that was a fair estimate of the situation.

The husky, red-bearded driver straightened. "Gonna have to cobble me up a new one. Time I get the critters tended and somethin' new whittled, be too dark to do much. Hafta stay here for the night. Shit."

When Fargo heard rustling behind him, he didn't see why the driver thought spending the night was such a bad idea.

Trying to be polite and helpful, Charlie stood by the coach door, helping the passengers step down. The first sported raven hair and so much bright rouge on her otherwise pale cheeks that she might have glowed in the dark. The next gal's henna rinse was even redder and brighter, and she showed plenty of well-turned leg to the helpful boy. Next came a brass-haired woman whose saffron dress boasted a low-scooped bodice that displayed her ample scenery, almost down to the nipples. If she'd had any more on top, she couldn't have stood up straight.

This was a coach full of whores, bound for the mining camps. Already they'd figured out that today's progress had ended. They were buzzing like a hive, making plans for the impromptu stopover. "I want that big jasper. Bet he can satisfy a lonesome gal." "Hey, I saw him first." "Who's to say he can't pleasure us both, Liz?" "You two can have him. I likes them young. No manners at all, but lots of energy." "Lemme give him a French lesson first, Dolly."

Amid the eight chattering trollops who'd stepped out, Charlie blushed furiously while several eyed him up and down. But he didn't look a bit displeased at the notion of spending the night here, guarding them or whatever. Fargo sure as hell wouldn't mind being a gentleman and helping out these poor women who didn't like to sleep in cold and lonely places.

Then the Trailsman remembered his job. "Shit." He turned to the driver. "Much as I'd like to stay here and help you out, I can't. We have to keep moving."

The stage driver gave Fargo a patronizing stare. "Ride on? You ain't playin' with no full deck, mister, if you just rides on and leaves all this. You must be soft in the head."

As they rode off, a wistful-looking Charlie kept turning and staring back.

Fargo knew he should have felt better about being so responsible to his job. But he, too, had a wistful countenance whenever he looked back, which was often.

7

Standing impatiently with their reins tied to the corral fence in the cool of a summer morning, the three horses looked edgy and ready to go. Fargo felt the same way when he left them and walked around past the stable to the front of the livery. He wished Charlie would get the hell back here after being sent off to buy a coil of grass rope. Now there was a damn crowd assembling out front. He scanned the group for the tall and skinny blond-haired kid.

Just about every other sort of humanity seemed to be represented here. Out in the dusty street between Denver's biggest livery stable and its stage station, folks of all sizes and ages stood, listening to the spiel that was coming from a tall frock-coated gent who stood on a soapbox, flanked by several helpers, two of them at a makeshift table assembled from planks supported by upended crates.

Maybe it was fitting that the smooth-tongued orator stood on a box that had once held soap, because that's what he was selling.

"Now, folks," he announced, holding up a cream-colored bar of soap about the size of his hand, "soap like this normally sells for about a nickel, right?" The crowd murmured agreement. "But as I shall demonstrate, you will soon be glad to pay a whole dollar, just for a piece of this bar."

From his vantage on the street edge of the boardwalk, about twenty feet from the soap salesman, Fargo again peered over the muttering group. A goodly number of the residents of Colorado Territory had so little use for soap that they wouldn't have been interested, even if the gent had been giving the stuff away. But this crowd didn't live here.

They were mostly people in his situation, just passing through, waiting for their stages to leave or visiting the stables to get ready for a trip. And Charlie was still not among them, dammit, so the Trailsman returned his attention to the speaker, who had by now finished slicing his soap into sixteen pieces with a penknife.

He waved a ten-dollar bill. "As you can see, I shall wrap this around one of these pieces of soap. Now, to make this proposition more interesting, we're going to wrap all these pieces of soap and set them on the table here." His assistants got busy with some brown wrapping paper and a pot of mucilage. "Any of you that feels lucky today, just step right up and buy a piece of soap for a dollar. And some of you are going to walk away with a real clean ten-dollar bill."

While the soap got wrapped and piled, and a line started to form, Fargo stood on tiptoes and eyed the crowd again. He was already taller than most men, and standing on the boardwalk, right where it dropped six inches to the powdery street, gave him even more of an edge. He had as good a view of the crowd as a man could get without climbing a ladder. And there was still no sign of Charlie.

Amid the jostling before him, the Trailsman couldn't help but notice how a short and roundish woman was now standing right in front of him. Likely she worked the dance halls, rather than the whorehouses, or she wouldn't have been out this early. But the little brunette would be popular wherever she went, thanks to the two pearly globes that stretched her bodice. It was cut so low that a man in front enjoyed a tantalizing view. From behind and above, where Fargo was watching, the sight was inspiring and more. He told the stirring in his trousers to behave itself and to quit bulging so.

Now that the orator had persuaded several dozen folks to start forming a line toward the tiny wrapped pieces of soap that stood piled on the plank table, his voice got more commanding. "I can see that some of you good people aren't interested yet, even with a chance to get ten dollars for one. So I have an even more profitable offer for your consideration." He reached into his broadcloth coat and triumphantly held out a crisp greenback worth a hundred dollars. "Watch careful, so you'll know I'm not cheating you." He wrapped it in soap and handed it to a confederate.

While Fargo enjoyed watching the gal in front of him breathe, he heard mutters that this had to be a confidence game, that there was no way in this world that the hundred-dollar chunk would end up on the table with the other soap. When the Trailsman raised his eyes, he saw Charlie, who must have edged into the crowd from down the street.

The gullible kid had heard enough to get into line, dammit. The Trailsman started to shout something, then thought better of it. A dollar was a cheap price to pay for a lesson in the ways of these gents that hustled crowds. Let the kid piss away a little money on this petty swindle, and then he'd know enough not to piss away a lot of money someday on a bigger scheme.

Fargo shifted his feet, partly for lack of anything better to do, but mostly to improve his view of the little lady's prominent twin charms. She shifted and straightened, too, so her bodice slipped down a bit. Fargo was trying to decide whether he was seeing a strawberry mottle or a sample of her areola when he felt the mildest of jostles from behind, followed by a grunted "Pardon me."

He spun. Nobody behind him was close enough to jostle, and the fat fellow he saw first, a step away, looked amazed and perplexed. Fargo's lake-blue eyes flitted. There he was, only a few steps away. Same son of a bitch he'd encountered up in Gouge-Eye, practicing the same trade. The Trailsman reached into his jacket, where there had been a little leather bag of coins, and the pocket was as empty as a politician's promise.

But the wiry man with such light fingers was only a few steps away. Cursing himself for paying too much attention to the lady's cleavage, and knowing that he'd miss the agreeable way her bosom rose and fell with each breath, Fargo started edging toward the pick-pocket. Slim didn't notice his approach, because he had a portly merchant with a tempting wallet almost within reach.

Fargo kept Slim in the corner of his vision while he looked over to see why the crowd was getting so noisy. Among the dozens of soap purchasers, three were waving ten-dollar bills. But it was Charlie who was the most excited. With the fifty-foot coil of rope hung over his shoulder, he was jumping up and down, crowing like a banty rooster. High over his head, he held the hundred-dollar greenback.

So much for that lesson, Fargo chuckled. It was the first time he'd ever seen anybody get the big money at one of these performances. But he had another lesson to give this morning, and the student was now almost within reach. Fargo politely sidestepped until he was right behind Slim. He was still on the edge of the plank sidewalk, blocking the view of some muttering folks behind him, and Slim stood down on the street, just a silent grab away from the merchant's wallet.

First things first, and what came first was recovering his own money. For a gent who, of all people, should have known better, Slim Boswick was surprisingly careless about such matters. Fargo spotted his leather bag in the right pocket of Slim's frayed, loose-fitting coat.

When Slim reached forward with his spidery right hand, Fargo reached forward with his big right hand. Slim got an easy pinch grip on the merchant's leather wallet. Fargo got a thumb-and-forefinger hold on the top of his leather bag. Slim's arm came up. So did Fargo's.

But Slim made his livelihood by being real sensitive, so he must have perceived how his baggy coat shifted on his shoulders after one pocket got lighter. He pivoted in a silent instant, his left hand coming around with a knife that was a lot like him—skinny, sharp, and mean-looking.

Fargo chopped down with his money bag. The hammer blow slammed into Slim's wrist. The fingers sprang open and the pigsticker knife fell to the street. Pain shot across Slim's clean-shaven face and registered in his beady brown eyes. His recent aquisition fell as he brought up his right hand, long fingers aimed at Fargo's eyes.

Fargo met that with his left and grabbed, his fingers now intertwined with Slim's. So far, this had been silent, since neither wanted to attract notice. Staying quiet was getting to be some work for Slim, though. His forehead furrowed and his eyes started to bulge as Fargo rolled the hand back, forcing Slim's wrist back to an impossible angle. Fargo figured that once Slim's skilled hand acquired a few shattered bones and ripped tendons, Slim might have to take up a new line of work. The Trailsman applied more pressure, bending the supple wrist back even more. Something would have to give soon.

What gave was Slim's silence. "Thief," he shouted. "Goddamn pickpocket."

Suddenly they were the center of attention. Slim kicked at the ground. "This sumbitch grabbed my bag." Fargo got his free hand up to Slim's thin-lipped mouth and felt a burly bystander tugging at his elbow. Slim went on, his toe now pointing at the wallet on the street. "Lookee here. He was busy grabbing that when I caught up to him."

Fargo whirled and shook his arm free while other bystanders grabbed at him. But it was only two bulling steps to the front wall of the livery, where he wouldn't have to worry about his back. Once he had his Colt out as he sidled along the wall, toward the front door, people did get a little more thoughtful about approaching him.

"Fetch the sheriff," somebody shouted. "Get the law after that big cutpurse." Slim Boswick didn't look pleased about that prospect, but he joined in the clamor as Fargo twisted through the front door and bounded through the office. He paused only to swing the bar after slamming shut the door between the front room and the stable.

The Trailsman sprinted toward the yawning back door, down the hallway flanked by stalls.

His thoughts raced as quickly as his feet. If he'd been traveling solo, he could jump on the Ovaro, all saddled and waiting just seconds away. The crowd of people on foot wouldn't have much chance of catching him, and by the time the local law could start after him, he'd be long gone. Not that Fargo really feared dealing with the law here, even now. The sheriff was reputedly a fair-minded gent who'd listen to reason. But squaring matters would take time, a day or two that Fargo didn't want to waste. Especially when that meant Charlie would be free to wander around Denver and discover more ways to wander off the straight and narrow.

But Fargo couldn't exactly ride out of town without Charlie, who was still out in front with his hundred-dollar bill. So the Trailsman swallowed glumly and figured he'd just have to talk to the sheriff. His bounding steps became a stroll by the time he reached the big barn door at the back.

Other than a couple dozen horses and mules, he didn't have any company in the corral. He stepped toward the Ovaro and sprang over the fence. He had the Ovaro's reins in his hand and the notion of leaving got as tempting as a woman's smile. It got more enchanting when he looked down the alley that led to the street and saw some people rushing his way.

The invasion wasn't a crowd, though. Just Charlie, his long legs stepping high and fast, with three men on his tail. They were part of the soap-selling crew. Two were bellowing that Charlie should best stop if he knew what was good for him. The front one, several yards behind Charlie and losing ground, was apparently trying to grab at his revolver and run at the same time.

Fargo waited until he could be sure the man's intentions were dishonorable. When the running man's pistol started up, Fargo's first round should have poked a hole in the man's chest, the best place when you needed to take down a running target.

But Charlie's leading pursuer slipped a bit on some fresh horse shit, so his head dropped some. The Trailsman's bullet plowed into his ear. The man stumbled forward, rocking sideways as a spray of blood, bone fragments, and maybe even brains erupted from his other ear. His two companions instantly flattened themselves, one to the ground behind the body, the other pressed against the whitewashed wall.

The boy, so intent on running that he almost passed the horses, vaulted atop his dappled gelding. Fargo jerked the reins loose from the fence rail and threw them to eager, trembling hands. "Get," he hollered. "I'll be along."

Charlie didn't need much urging, and neither did the gelding when several shots roared out of the alley. The two men back there were grifters, Fargo knew, men who disdained robbery at gunpoint because swindling was so much safer and easier. When they used their guns, it was generally just for show, and always at close range. So he wasn't too concerned that they'd hit much of anything. Just to make them more nervous, he sent two close shots their way, turning from his saddle as he did so.

Since he was a kid who didn't know his way around, Charlie had naturally ridden straight out of town in the dumbest possible direction. North or south, there was the South Platte River, where they could hole up along the tree-shaded banks for the rest of the day, until Denver settled down. West, the prairie started turning into mountains, and in the roughening country, you could lose anybody except a real good and persistent tracker. A posse hastily assembled for a pickpocket wasn't likely to boast much in the way of talent or persistence.

But dead east, there was nothing but short-grass prairie for at least a hundred miles. Most of this land was flat as a griddle, and fixing to get damn near as hot once the sun climbed a little higher. Fargo prodded the Ovaro and caught up to Charlie, whose horse led the roan pack mare in a loping trot that stirred up a big rooster tail of dust.

"I remembered the rope, Mr. Fargo," was all that Charlie could think of to say when the Trailsman drew abreast.

"Glad to see that," Fargo replied. He looked back to see whether they'd inspired a posse, and all he could see was sagebrush and brown buffalo grass under a swirling tan haze of dust. "You want to explain why those soap salesmen were so damn eager to catch you?"

Charlie winced and looked shamefaced while licking his dust-caked lips.

"Don't do that. Just get a mouth full of mud, and your lips'll crack and bleed," Fargo cautioned. "Now, I don't have a switch in my hand, and there aren't any woodsheds hereabouts. So you're not going to get a whipping, no matter what happened back in Denver. But I'd sure like to know. It could make a considerable difference in our travel plans."

Charlie'd had no trouble buying the rope at the hardware store three blocks away. On his way back to the stable, he'd run into one of the smooth-talking soap men.

"The man offered me a double-eagle if'n I'd do a little chore for him. Said it wouldn't take but a few minutes, and I didn't reckon we were in all that big a hurry. So I took him up on it, and he give me the twenty dollars. Got it in my pocket if you want to see it."

Fargo shook his head and turned in the saddle. Damn the dust. No way to see what was coming behind them unless they'd stopped for a spell, and it was too soon for that. Fargo turned back to Charlie. "What was the chore?"

"I was to stand in line and buy a wrapped chunk of soap from him. He said it'd have money in the wrapping. I was supposed to wave it around and then give him the money back afterward."

The horses were trotting easy, and Fargo studied on prodding them into a gallop. But there wasn't any percentage in working the horses any harder than necessary, especially out in this desolation. "Guess they managed to palm the soap slivers so you got the right one, because I saw you waving that greenback, just when I got in my ruckus. What happened?"

"Well, I seen you in trouble, so I started legging it toward you. Didn't know what I'd do, but it did appear you were in a bind, Mr. Fargo. Plumb forgot about that gent's money. Guess he didn't, though."

Charlie paused, started to lick his lips, caught Fargo's glare, and pulled his tongue in. "You wasn't really picking a pocket, was you, Mr. Fargo?"

The Trailsman pulled out his bandanna and wiped some of the sweat and dust off his face before answering. "Matter of fact, I was. Slim Boswick grabbed my leather pouch while I was distracted by, well, by the soap palaver. So I eased over to steal it back from him. Just got it when he spun and hollered that I was the pickpocket. Things got a little hectic after that."

They pounded on for a minute or two before Charlie responded. "I knowed you weren't no crook, Mr. Fargo. Guess I am, though. I've still got that gent's money."

"Don't feel too bad about it, Charlie. Ain't like that fellow earned it honest. They were just using you to shill the crowd, to make folks think their badger game wasn't crooked."

"But some folks were gettin' ten-dollar bills they could keep."

"Charlie, you've got a good head for numbers. Use it for a damn minute."

When his thoughtful countenance turned into a big dust-streaked grin, the boy turned back to the Trailsman. "I see how it works," he said. "You sells sixteen slivers of soap at a buck apiece. Even if'n it's honest and there's a sawbuck in every batch, which there ain't, that's sixteen dollars in for every ten that goes out. Less the nickel for the bar of soap, of course, and maybe two cents for the wrapping paper. That's a pretty good-paying proposition. My dad says if you get twenty percent on your money over a year, it's a worthwhile investment, and these gents were getting nigh sixty percent in less than an hour."

He closed his eyes for about a minute. "Why, Mr. Fargo, if you started with a hundred dollars and ten bars of soap, and worked it so you sold ten cut-up bars every day for a year, you'd end up with twenty-one thousand, six hundred and forty-four dollars and fifty cents to the good."

"Sounds about right," an amazed Fargo agreed. The countryside wasn't quite as flat as it looked, for they were climbing a gentle rise. "Let's rein up here and see if we can calculate whether anybody's after us."

Once the drifting dust settled under their short shadows, Fargo scanned the prairie. In three directions there was nothing but clear air and pungent sagebrush. Back the way they'd come, toward the west, the land sloped gently toward Denver, which shimmered in the distance, seven or eight miles away. Behind the settlement rose the Front Range of the Rocky Mountains in gray-blue majesty, clawing at the big white puffball clouds that floated through the deep-blue sky.

In front of Denver, toward them, swirled a brown plume. Leisurely riding didn't tend to stir that much dust. Wagon trains didn't move fast, although they churned up considerable clouds that generally hung low and extended for a mile or two, like big wriggling snakes. This was more like a column than a cloud, about what you'd expect from a tight-knit group of hard-ridden horses. A pursuing posse of about a dozen men would raise dust just that way.

"Shit," Fargo muttered. "Didn't reckon the good folks of Denver would get that enthusiastic about chasing a mere pickpocket."

"Didn't you have your gun out? Wasn't there some shots fired?" Charlie asked as he dismounted to take a leak, as long as they were stopped anyway.

"That did happen," Fargo confessed, "but it'd seem to me that they'd just figure on good riddance for that soap seller I had to stop before he got a shot at you. But mayhaps those swindlers were sharing some of their ample profits with the local law. In which case, the sheriff just might take this serious and act like it was an honest citizen, instead of a grifter, that just got killed."

His back to Fargo, Charlie turned his head. "You killed a man on account of me?"

"Guess that's one way to put it," Fargo said. "Hope there's some way out of this without killing any more, or getting us both killed."

As they resumed the back-jarring trot, the Trailsman studied on what they might do.

Hiding wasn't impossible, even on what looked like featureless prairie. Many a white rider had come across such a stretch, sure that he was alone. As one of his last acts on this earth, he'd discover that an empty patch of shortgrass and sagebrush could conceal several dozen Indians. The Comanche could even hide horses out in this stuff. They had a trick to get their mounts to lie flat in the tiny swales created by buffalo that sometimes rolled in the dust to discourage the flies on their backs.

But Charlie was an impatient kid who'd get edgy after about two minutes of such hunkering, so that was out unless it became absolutely necessary. Even then, Fargo figured he'd have to knock the kid cold to have much hope of avoiding discovery.

They had a good start on the pursuing posse. But that didn't mean much, because Fargo and Charlie's own little plume of dust would be in plain sight from back there, at least for whoever was leading the group. The dust would announce just where they were, what direction they were heading, how fast they were going, and all the other things you like to know when you're trying to catch somebody.

Maybe ride to some better cover, where they might stand off or evade the posse until they might sneak out under cover of darkness. But for twenty miles, there wasn't enough shade to keep a jackrabbit from sweating, unless they rode straight back to Denver, right into the posse.

Fargo searched his memory. Had he ever been out here before? One chunk of this prairie looked pretty much like any other, and the farther east you went, the harder it was to use the distant haze-shrouded mountains for landmarks.

No, he decided, he hadn't. He'd crossed the Great Plains many times, using one of two common routes to reach Denver from what passed for civilization in Missouri. Neither of them came at the city from this direction. But there was also a trail that ran pretty much due east of Denver. By better than a hundred miles, it offered the shortest connection to civilization. It reached the Smoky Hill River somewhere near the line that separated Colorado Territory from Kansas Territory.

They'd strike that trail within an hour if they kept heading this way. Along its route, they might find some cover for discouraging the posse—an abandoned wagon, perhaps, or a ruined sod hut. Fargo wasn't too sure what might be found, because he'd never been there. Avoiding such places was one reason he was still alive.

Back in 1859, at the start of the Gold Rush, the trail had been a popular route. For about six weeks. Then the truth began to emerge about how desolate this region really was. No trees for fuel or shelter. There wasn't grass worth mentioning. For long stretches, water was limited to what you could carry. So was food, as those who planned on hunting game discovered that buffalo and antelope were harder to find than honest men at a lawyers' convention. About all you could find out there were surly Cheyenne war parties, and they found you, generally with arrows or lances.

In honor of the sporadic river out along its eastern end, the route had been christened the Smoky Hill Trail. Folks who'd been across it once—few ever took the Smoky Hill twice, and a dismaying proportion didn't even live through their first try—sometimes called it the Thirst Road or the Starvation Trail. But mostly it was known as the Smoky Hell Trail.

Some ruts swung up from the south. The Trailsman and the kid continued their trot.

Ahead of him, as far to the east as Fargo cared to look, the remnants of the murderous Smoky Hill Trail stretched to the east. No more than an hour behind them to the west rode a trigger-happy posse. North and south was just desolation until your horse gave out. Then you'd give out, and the best you could hope was that the coyotes would feel properly grateful for the meal your desiccated corpse would provide. Fargo didn't see that they had much choice but to keep going.

8

"Mr. Fargo, why for are we stopping so often when we got a posse hot after us?"

The Trailsman savored the mouthful of tepid water before allowing it to trickle down his parched throat. He grudgingly moved the canteen from his lips and carefully replaced its cap before answering. This was no thirst-quencher, just a dust-cutter to keep a man's mouth from clogging up.

"Charlie, we don't dare push the horses too hard."

"But from that dust cloud, it looks like they're a-gainin' plenty on us." Charlie took the canteen. He'd paid careful mind to Fargo's swallow, and took his sip, although it was obvious that he was fighting a strong urge to drain the vessel in one gulp.

"For a while, maybe. But horses work about the same as we do. The harder you run them, the sooner they get tuckered out. Those boys will slow down considerable soon, and we'll still be moving. We don't have to stay much ahead—just out of rifle range, as far as that goes. And if we're still ahead by sundown, our posse worries are likely over."

Charlie replaced the canteen in its saddle pouch and pulled off his broad-brimmed hat to fan his sweaty, dust-caked face. "Why would that be?"

"You study on that while we move on," the Trailsman replied, swinging into his saddle. From his higher perch, Fargo surveyed the terrain. A lot of nothing, except for the posse cloud about five miles back. Overhead, the sun was working about as hard as it ever did, although the drifting cumulus clouds had lost their fleecy look as they started to swell, darken, and bunch up. On the baked, desolate ground, Fargo and Charlie still trended uphill, even though they were headed away from the mountains.

That was one of the curiosities of the West that Fargo had always wanted to inquire about. From the Mississippi westward, the plains rose gently, like a tilted table. You'd expect them to continue like that right on up to the mountains. But instead, about seventy miles east of the Front Range, just when the mountains came into view from the east, the land began to drop, down into a long trough that ran parallel to the east wall of the Rockies.

It didn't seem at all reasonable, but Fargo reckoned that if he'd been in charge of laying out the earth, he'd have done a lot of things in a more sensible way. Like put some grass, water, and shade out here.

"I got it, Mr. Fargo," Charlie interjected. "That posse was rounded up in a hurry. They figured on just riding out a few miles. So they likely ain't equipped to spend the night out here. Even if they do, most of 'em are just jaspers that got other work back in Denver they'd want to tend to. So they're apt to turn back afore too long, bein' as we didn't do nothin' all that serious."

"Go to the head of the class," Fargo answered, recalling that teaching the boy how to escape lawful posses probably wasn't exactly what Darius Hamilton had had in mind for this excursion.

After their next stop, an hour or so later, the land lost its monotonous aspect. Rocks began to mingle with the sand beneath them. The countryside became more broken, chopped up by gulches and draws. Some had steepish walls, but none ran more than a dozen feet deep. From the look of them, they'd been carved out about the time Noah launched his ark, and hadn't seen water since. The Trailsman pursued his usual course through such country, riding just below the ridgeline, which was the trail's general course, too. That way, the gulches generally weren't deep or steep enough to matter, and you didn't give anybody an easy skyline shot at you.

But he was worried. Charlie's mount was starting to favor its near front foot. The damn dappled gelding wasn't really a bad horse, considering, but it did seem to be trouble-prone. Some people were like that, too. They meant well. It wasn't like they went out of their way to make life difficult for folks around them. But they somehow brought complication wherever they went. "Charlie, rein up and dismount."

He did, a question starting to show under the sweat-streaked dust.

Fargo got his in first. "You notice anything peculiar about the way that gelding was riding?"

"For the past mile or so, reckon he swayed more'n usual, now that I think about it. Why?"

"Charlie, you've got to pay mind to such things soon as you notice them. Horses don't talk none too well. The only way a horse can tell you that there might be a problem is with its body, like when it starts walkin' different."

The boy nodded and crouched next to Fargo, holding the gelding's reins. The Trailsman had the horse's favored leg bent back, so the hoof was up. A sharp chunk of trail rock, about the size of a thumbnail, was wedged in the tender fleshy spot between the frog and the sole. Fargo flicked at it and saw the horse quiver while the offending rock remained in place.

The Trailsman reached for his belt knife. He'd have to hold the upturned hoof with one hand and dig the rock out while Charlie held the gelding's reins. But if the horse got skittish, which could happen easy . . . No, that wouldn't be wise. Charlie wasn't that skilled at handling contrary horses, and they could both end up getting pummeled by hooves.

Fargo lifted his eyes to meet the boy's. "Reckon we could swap places, and I hold while you dig out this rock, nice and gentle?"

"Sure, Mr. Fargo. I've done that afore." The boy wasn't bragging, either. Fargo held tight, making sure the gelding knew that it was going to get choked or shot if it so much as flicked its tail. Next to him, Charlie crouched, one hand around the upside-down hoof while the other worked the knife. He took his time, maybe more time than he should have, going easy as he probed with the tip and worried the rock out. The boy even looked close after it was out to see if the rock had amounted to anything more than an irritation, which it hadn't.

But that was the damn problem with having folks after you. Had that happened to one of the posse, the gent could just drop back, tend to his mount, and catch up or turn back, as the spirit struck him. The posse would keep moving toward its prey. But Charlie and Fargo hadn't gone anywhere for the better part of an hour, and now they could damn near smell the dust churned up by their pursuers.

No, that wasn't dust the Trailsman sensed. It was a change in the air. He scanned the sky. Shit and double shit. Those fluffy clouds were now looming anvil-shaped thunderheads, fixing to swallow the sun at any moment. The color of a bad bruise, they promised rain.

Not that this parched country couldn't use some moisture, all it could get. But riding in the wet got tiresome, and besides, Fargo didn't know just how much Charlie might tolerate after his last bout with the chilling rains that pounded their coldness into a man's hide.

Riding was kind of a dumb notion anyway, if those clouds, now providing welcome relief from the heat as they rolled in front of the sun, began to cut loose with lightning. Thunderbolts tended to strike the high spots, and out here, a man on a horse rose about as high as anything did. Fargo eyed the dappled gelding under Charlie and wondered just how soon it might spook this time around.

Avoiding the lightning by hunkering down in a ravine could be foolish, too, on account of flash floods. But they were close to some sort of dividing ridge. If they didn't go too far down before they crawled in under a cut bank, then there just wouldn't be enough of a catch basin above them to make a whole lot of flood. Maybe.

If there was one easy way to cope with thunderstorms on the prairie, Fargo had sure never discovered it. Sharp gusts whistled through the Trailsman's beard, followed in moments by a few spatters.

Fargo turned the Ovaro downhill, toward a likely

draw that extended to the north. Charlie followed, asking about their changed direction while swirling wind ripped the words from his mouth. Fierce rain buffeted them before they'd ridden a quarter of a mile, toward a steep-sided spot where they might find some cover.

Not much cover, though. Although the draw sported near-vertical walls, it was at least twenty yards wide, and those walls were maybe ten feet high. The gulch itself wouldn't offer any protection. But during some earlier cloudburst, the floodwater had surged around a bend to carve out an overhang. It didn't go back even a full arm's length. The hollowed-out spot was maybe a yard high, and a little wider.

One man might crouch in it, if he didn't mind acquiring a fearsome backache. Two could sit inside, if they didn't mind stretching their legs out into the open. Even at that, just how much shelter they'd enjoy depended on which way the wind was coming. If from their back, they'd be cozy. If from the way they faced, they might as well not have bothered. The overhang's very existence meant that it wasn't a real safe place for hiding from a storm; if the water had roared high and fast enough once to create the hollow, then another sudden flood could certainly rip through there again.

Squinting through the rain, Fargo mulled on that for a moment. Maybe they should look for something better. The weather made up his mind for him as he felt buckshot pelt his shoulders. It wasn't buckshot, though, just hail pellets plunging down from that booming, exploding darkness overhead. Like it or not, this was the place.

Trying to ignore how the hailstones were gaining size and velocity by the moment, Fargo jerked his saddle off the Ovaro. Without asking, Charlie struggled to do likewise with his gelding, which wasn't at all pleased by another exploding thunderstorm. The horse hadn't spooked yet, but its eyes were drawn wide and its ears flared.

Fargo hollered at Charlie, but his words were lost in the rising clamor of clacking hailstones. Precariously balancing the saddle over his head for protection, he stepped over to Charlie.

"Get in there," he hollered, pointing at the overhang about ten yards away. He pulled the boy in under the dripping saddle. "Stay under this till you get there." He shifted and crouched a bit, so that Charlie's head was now in the center of their make-do umbrella. The boy had to use one hand to steady it as the hail pounded against its top. The Trailsman shoved the Ovaro's reins into the boy's other hand. "Hold these."

After grabbing the gray's reins and jamming them under his gun belt, with hopes that that would keep the skittish mount from lighting out, Fargo ducked so that Charlie could swing the overhead saddle around and take off for the overhang.

Under the saddle, the hail had only sounded bad. Now it was hitting bad. Most stones in this fusillade were the size of marbles, stinging like hornets as they assaulted the Trailsman's broad shoulders.

His broad-brimmed and high-crowned hat offered some protection, though. His hands got hammered as he struggled with the pack mare's tether, finally persuading the knot on the rain-swelled rope to come loose. He looped it around the front buck on the packsaddle and swatted the mare on the rear. Just how it knew it was being swatted was a mystery, the way the hail was thudding against its hide, but it did kick up its heels and hurry up the draw.

The mare was lost in the streaks of rain and hail as the Trailsman pulled his stinging hands to his face, under the shelter of the hat brim, and blew on them. That didn't warm them much. They still felt as stiff as sticks when he leaned against the gelding and reached for its cinch ring.

He'd just gotten a grip on the latigo, slippery like soap in this rain, when the gelding got even more worried, suddenly tensing. No lightning or thunder, no more than usual, anyway. Fargo's eyes flitted across the nearby ground. Nothing there, except for hail, which was starting to pile up. Already the prairie was cloaked in white.

It was all bouncing furiously, almost like so much popcorn in a skillet, and some spots resembled eruptions. A streak from the sky would strike, spraying ice up and out, leaving a little crater for a few moments.

The gelding tensed and winced again, as if someone had just clubbed it with an ax handle. Bent against the horse's side, Fargo ignored that and cussed some more at the way that wet rigging got impossible to work with.

Then he knew why the gelding acted so proddy about just having to stand there. A hammer slammed the small of Fargo's back. A couple inches up and over, and it would have been a rabbit punch to make a dirty fighter proud. As it was, it damn near knocked his wind out, and he sagged against the horse, still struggling with the latigo. There, it was coming undone. Next thing, somebody dropped an anvil on his shoulder.

Gritting his teeth and continuing to look downward while the pain clawed down his arm and surged toward his chest, the Trailsman saw the fist-sized clump of ice that must have broken something up on the top of his arm. The limb stung and his hand and fingers didn't want to obey orders. Finally, the damn rigging came loose.

Now, to swing the mess over his head, before he caught one of those monster hailstones with his skull. His hat protected from the little stuff that came earlier, but beaver felt would not keep him from getting knocked cold if one of these giants smashed into its crown. Maybe this was the time for a suit of armor, but he'd have to make do with a saddle.

The Trailsman gripped the saddle and got it overhead, steadying it with his right hand. With his left, he jerked the gelding's reins and threw them over the horse's heaving withers. It didn't need a swat for encouragement as it followed the vanished roan on up the draw.

Before he could get the saddle steadied with his left hand so he could pull his right in, another huge stone smashed his hand, with such force that his fingers sprang open. The slick saddle slipped as he twisted underneath, trying to keep it balanced on his head while his feet fought for firm footing. It was like trying to stay up on an ice-skating pond covered with greased marbles.

Unable to keep his feet under him, Fargo let nature take its course, staying in control as much as he could as he fell. He landed with the saddle over his head, and legs stuck out where one kneecap got walloped by what felt like a sledgehammer. The throbbing joint complained mightily about having to bend after that blow, but he finally got crouched under the saddle.

His hands, one still unwilling to let him close it all the way, gripped the insides of the fenders. He stood. Nothing fell off, even when a sizable stone slammed the seat right over his head, so hard that he felt the jolt all the way down his spine. Although he desperately wanted to hurry, the Trailsman stepped deliberately toward the overhang, just a dim outline through the streaks of rain and hail.

Right behind the Ovaro's saddle, Charlie huddled against the sand and rocks, scrunched up and terrified. But he still had a white-fingered death grip on the Ovaro's reins.

Fargo now knew what boulders felt like after they'd been through a stamp mill. This was worse than being on bottom in a logging-camp brawl where everybody wore hobnailed boots. Still holding a saddle overhead, he kicked the one at his feet, his own, until it was lined up with Charlie.

The heavens hadn't been at all cooperative for the past thirty minutes, but Fargo figured he could thank heaven for one little favor. Charlie had figured out what to do. He had slumped back, pushing his back to the wall while he stuck his legs out under the saddle. That left enough room, just barely, for the Trailsman to sit the same way, his legs protected by the gelding's saddle.

Now their heads and torsos could stay pretty well out of the assault from the sky. Their legs had to stick out, of course, but under the saddles, their extended limbs were sheltered, even as the hail came thicker and bigger.

The soaked and bedraggled Ovaro obviously wanted to be somewhere else, since he was getting his stuffing pounded out of him. If one of those big stones hit him between the ears, he might even get knocked out. Fargo sympathized with his old friend, but those were the breaks. If this storm ever ended, they'd need one horse at hand to use to catch the others.

Past the battered Ovaro, rain-formed pools along the sandy bottom were starting to connect, floating hailstones along a rippling muddy flow already a yard wide. The Trailsman and the kid sat on a bench maybe two feet above the bottom, where the water was commencing to flow in earnest, but the sight was still worrisome.

"Mr. Fargo, what're we gonna do if'n that water starts gettin' much higher?" Even though they sat shoulder to shoulder, the thunder, hail, and rain made so much racket that Charlie had to turn his head and almost shout in Fargo's ear.

"Shuck our duds and swim for it, maybe," Fargo replied, knowing it wasn't much of an answer. If the hail didn't stop and this vicious rain continued, they faced a choice between drowning and getting beaten to death. It wasn't something the Trailsman cared to talk about. If and when the time came, he'd fret about his options then.

After what seemed like an eternity, the hail gave up. It didn't ease up, or taper down from those fist-sized stones to something more reasonable. It just stopped. One second the shaking surface of the earth was getting whiter by the moment, and the next, all that the sky poured out was the refreshingly soft and liquid rain.

The rain held on for a few more minutes, slowing at an almost imperceptible rate, as if it knew that since it seldom visited these parts, it just had to stay for just as long as it could. But finally the downpour waned to a few harmless sprinkles. Fargo pulled his long legs out from under the dripping saddle and stepped over to the Ovaro. His boots crunched through four or five inches of accumulated hail with each step.

He ran his hands carefully across the pinto's back

and sides. Since horses' hides were covered with hair, bruises and similar tender spots didn't generally show. You had to feel your way along, noting every time the horse tensed or quivered. Which happened pretty often. There wasn't going to be any comfortable way to hang a saddle on the pinto stallion; he'd need a day or two of rest and liniment before he'd be in any shape for hard travel.

But there was work that had to be done now, whether the Ovaro liked it or not. For all that, Fargo would have preferred a feather bed next to a warm stove now, too. His smashed right hand still complained about closing its fingers, his bruised back throbbed with every breath, and his knee felt stiffer than a ramrod.

Trying to ignore his sensible desire to crawl off somewhere with a bottle, Fargo called back to Charlie to stay reasonably put, then swung aboard bareback. If he didn't fetch their other two horses now, they might get frisky and decide to sample the grass of Nebraska or New Mexico before he caught up to them.

Up on the ridge, as the wrung-out clouds wandered east with the breeze, the Trailsman looked back to the west. No dust clouds to make observation simple, so he had to strain some. About two miles off, flat out in an open area, the posse struggled to reassemble itself.

He was too distant to be absolutely sure what was going on, but it was pleasant to guess. All the horses were still rigged, which meant that the men hadn't known the plainsmen's trick of using their saddles as shelter during hailstorms. About half the men were able to sit up in their saddles; the others, who were knocked-out or maybe worse, had been thrown across their saddles, and their horses were being led. The group started back to Denver at a listless pace.

It was perhaps small comfort to see that other folks had fared worse with the hail than he had. But comfort was like shelter, Fargo reckoned. Sometimes you had to settle for what you could get. And it was big comfort to know that their pummeled posse was giving up the chase.

The mare and the gelding had wandered only as far

as the next draw, where Fargo found them standing in front of what looked like a cave. It was really just an overhang like his and Charlie's, but this one went back better than a dozen feet. Most of the way, it was high enough for the Trailsman to stand straight in. A couple of fresh plops on its dry and sandy floor confirmed that the two horses had been considerably more comfortable during the hailstorm than he'd been.

No wonder the two horses lifted their thirsty heads out of a pool and seemed to grin at him in such a sassy way. The Trailsman left his battered Ovaro at the pool and swung aboard the gelding, leading the haltered roan back to Charlie. The featureless western horizon was going to catch up to the sun in about an hour, and this big overhang was as good a place as any to spend the night.

Greasewood made a tolerable cooking fire for the cottontail Fargo plunked with his Colt. While they devoured it, the Trailsman considered what came next, now that they didn't have a posse right behind them.

The eroding ruts of the Smoky Hill Trail rolled on eastward, not a quarter-mile from where they sat, and they were headed that way anyway. The main reason to take some other route was the lack of water along that trail, and the thunderstorm meant that there'd be wet spots for at least a couple days, maybe longer. Three or four days of hard riding would get them into Kansas, far enough to where the grass and water were consistent.

They had food to carry them twice that long, in a pinch. Figuring they'd take some sensible route, with trading posts and the like, or teeming with overburdened pioneers happy to shed some of their cargo as they struggled westward, Fargo hadn't packed as much as he might have otherwise. But there was only so much you could put on a packhorse, anyway, and make any kind of time.

So heading east on the Smoky Hill Trail made more sense than veering forty miles north to the Platte or a hundred south to the Arkansas. Those routes wandered all over hell and back after that, too.

The Ovaro, outside rolling in the mud to salve his

hidden bruises, wasn't in any condition for hard riding, though, and wouldn't be for a couple days. By then the land would again be dry. But if they shifted their gear to make the pack rig light as possible, and put that atop the Ovaro while Fargo rode the mare or the gelding, the big pinto would manage well enough.

Despite its justly earned and disgusting reputation, the Smoky Hill was the shortest route to Missouri, and Fargo had by now decided he wanted to get this job done as soon as reasonably possible. As kids went, Charlie wasn't bad company. But behaving himself around the boy was getting tiresome. Right now he could use a soothing shot of whiskey, and he didn't see that his thirst was going to slacken.

Besides that, keeping the curious and good-natured kid away from temptation would be a lot easier if they weren't around people. Since nobody ever rode the Smoky Hill these days, they weren't likely to encounter many tinhorns, fancy gals, dance halls, saloons, roadhouses, and the like. At least, so it seemed.

9

The Trailsman tugged his twisted hat brim even lower, trying to keep the glaring and malicious rising red sun out of his eyes. The roan's swaying and unfamiliar gait provided enough discomfort on its own, and the high cantle of his saddle didn't help, because it kept jabbing at the bruise that a big hailstone had left low on his back. One knee still throbbed every time a hoof fell. His right hand argued back whenever he told it to close enough to grip the reins. This was about as bad as any hangover he'd ever suffered, and the worst of it was that he'd somehow missed the pleasure of getting drunk first.

Charlie pulled up abreast and asked if they were now on the infamous Smoky Heck Trail.

The Trailsman allowed that the boy was free to cuss all he wanted in his company, within reason, and confirmed that they were indeed riding the Smoky Hell.

"When we come out here on a wagon train a couple years ago, we took the Smoky Hell." The boy's emphasis on the end of his sentence showed just how much he relished using such words around adults. "But this don't look familiar."

They were crossing the same sort of busted-up prairie as yesterday afternoon, and from where they rode to the end of the visible earth, in any direction, there wasn't anything else.

"Even out here, things look different, depending on which way you're headed," Fargo explained. "That's one reason you look behind you a lot, even when there's no posse after you. That way, if you come back over the same route, you know how it's supposed to look."

There was another reason to be looking in every direction. Actually, two reasons: Cheyenne, and Arapaho. But no sense bringing that up at the moment.

"Reckon so, Mr. Fargo. It's a caution how much you know about riding through wilderness. How long'd it take you to learn all that?"

"About as long as I've been alive, Charlie. This isn't some school where they give you a diploma when they decide they've filled you up. Every day, I learn something new just by keeping my eyes open. And it pays to be especially mindful when you're in new country, like today. Sounds like you're the experienced hand on the Smoky Hell."

"But not this stretch," Charlie protested. "Reckon that somewhere out east of here, where the sand got real bad, they swung south some on our trip, because I remember a lot of hoorah when we struck Cherry Creek. Mom was right pleased, because it was the first decent water for quite a stretch. Lot of alkali seeps along there that tasted funny. Horse and oxen didn't seem to mind, but it made a lot of folks sick, and her sicker than most." He tried to pretend that he had something in his eye, to obscure the tears that came up when he thought of Lydia Hamilton.

Fargo shifted the subject a bit. "Anything else about the route you took? Long dry stretches? Good grass somewhere? Indian troubles?"

"Nothin' peculiar. I kind of liked it, just rolling along, gettin' to drive the wagon now and again. Nobody seemed all that fretful, considering what I've heard since about the Smoky Hell. But we sure traveled with a ton of food, and we filled them water barrels every chance we got."

"Remember your guide? That's the kind of work I generally do."

" 'Course I remember Mr. Davis. Mr. Josh Davis. He let me ride up ahead with him once, the day we struck the forks of the Smoky Hill."

Fargo scanned the empty land. Aside from the ruts they followed, there wasn't any evidence that anyone had ever been here. Up above, the sky glowed blue and brilliant, unmarred by any clouds. Once the world heated up, they'd have to find a leftover rain pool somewhere for the horses, and take a three- or four-hour nooning. "I know Josh. He's a fair hand at this trade."

"Well, he did allow that he was pretty damn good. Maybe the best, though he confessed that a gent named Skye Fargo was about as good as they came if you couldn't hire Josh Davis. He seemed to know his business. You ever seen the forks of the Smoky Hill River?"

Fargo shook his head. "Crossed it farther down many times."

"Well, we rode up to them forks. The north one was runnin' a decent head of water, and the south one just dribbled and spit some. I woulda bet cash money that we'd take the north one. Anybody would. But he headed us south."

"Find out why?" Fargo already knew that if there was a chance for Charlie to ask a question, he'd ask it, but what the hell. It wasn't like they had much else to do except shoot the breeze.

"Seems that the north fork only goes for about twenty miles, to some springs. Past that, there's nothin' to it. Along the south, there ain't much water, and sometimes we had to dig for it in the dry creek bed, but we always found some when we needed it. Mr. Fargo, how's a man to know somethin' like that?"

"By getting lost and thirsty himself a few times," Fargo explained, "and by asking a lot of questions if you run into folks who've been across that country. I suppose it'd be a lot simpler if we had maps."

"There are maps and guidebooks, Mr. Fargo." Charlie paused for a moment. "But Mr. Davis said none of 'em was worth a plugged nickel in hell. He said there were some fellers in Kansas that published one certain guidebook, one that sent people up the north fork an' said there was good grass and easy water all the way to the gold fields. He said those lying sacks of shit ought to be horsewhipped, and then strung up for murder."

Fargo raised his estimate of his chief competitor in a

good-natured rivalry. Getting a wagon train across the Smoky Hell in 1859 without undue incident was a fine piece of work, something that Fargo would have been proud to brag on if he'd been the one to do it. Of course, taking the Smoky Hell, when there were more sensible, if longer, routes, didn't indicate any abundance of good judgment. He'd have to rawhide Josh some about that next time their paths crossed.

Fargo and Charlie swapped tall tales for a spell, until the sun got high and the heat started to show on the horses. The Trailsman nudged the roan toward a fair-sized pool that shimmered half a mile away, down off the trail in a swale. Heartened by the prospect of some more mud to roll in, the Ovaro trotted right along, trailing on his tether. The gelding looked eager enough, too, but apprehension showed on Charlie's face.

The boy kept squinting toward the water while they rode toward it. Finally he said something.

"Mr. Fargo, there's somethin' moving down there."

Since he'd been scanning the barren countryside, Fargo missed the motion by the pond. He looked hard as they approached. Some half-submerged reedy weeds showed the pond had risen some on account of yesterday's rain. They also indicated that the pool generally held some water, reasonably good water if all the churned-up mud at its edge meant anything.

In dry country, the water that looked cleanest—wasn't muddy and wasn't rimmed by weeds and scat from various animals—was almost certainly the worst. Animals and plants avoided such pure-looking water because it carried poisons like alkali, selenium, and arsenic. Alkali wasn't too hard to spot, because the nearby soil would be coated with a slick, chalklike residue. For the others, you just had to reckon that if the coyotes didn't think the water was fit to drink, you'd best avoid it too.

Even as they drew within steps of the pool, the Trailsman couldn't see whatever Charlie said he'd seen. Nothing moved down there. But the boy was still staring across the water, all of ten yards from their edge, toward a tangle of brush. Fargo heard something crackle over there and caught the motion, first in the scant leaves, then below. Likely it was just a cottontail scatting about under such cover as it could find in the harsh noonday glare.

A rabbit would sit fine for lunch, though, Fargo told Charlie as they halted at the edge of the mud and pulled the packsaddle off the bruised Ovaro. Their mounts could stay rigged, but the hail-battered pinto needed all the relief they could give him. They took turns, one holding the horses while the other went down for a drink, and they let the horses go stomp around and muddy up the pool while they drank their fill.

The horses weren't going to wander off for any distance, not with water and some green grass right here. But every time they started around the pool, they snorted and bristled their ears and backed off. The Ovaro insisted on taking his mud bath right in front of the little slope where the two humans sat. Fargo had figured on waiting a spell before going over to see the rabbit about lunch, but the horses found something annoying as hell about the spot that Charlie kept glancing it.

"Let's go see what's over there," the Trailsman finally announced. "It's got the horses as stirred up as you are."

Charlie looked dubious. "I can wait here, Mr. Fargo."

"Charlie, if it was something that could hurt us, it'd done it by now. Come on." They legged it around the pool, staying high to avoid the mud until they got above the brush. A path of sorts, like the trail of something being dragged, had been worn through the cactus and bunchgrass, leading to the brush. The area held a mild town stench of rot and privies, a stink that didn't belong on these wind-scoured prairies.

Fargo drew his Colt and glanced over at Charlie. No wonder the kid looked like he wanted to stay put. He didn't have a gun. Somewhere between here and civilization, Fargo decided, they'd find a revolver, or maybe a carbine, for Charlie, and he'd teach the boy to use it. With all that could happen on these trips, it was foolishness to be traveling with somebody that wasn't armed.

"Okay, stay put," Fargo intoned, then stepped toward the brush. He heard a croak, except it didn't sound like a frog's.

There. Almost at his feet. A man lying in the brush. More dead than alive, but still live enough to try lifting his bone-thin arm at Fargo's approach. He croaked hoarsely again.

After sweeping back the brush, Fargo knelt by his sunburned head. The man stank considerable, from lying in his own excrement and from the open sores that showed through the tatters of his clothes. Where the frayed shirt didn't hide them, his ribs showed, and his elbows stuck out like knots along the flesh that sagged from his sticklike arms. Some fresh bruises showed that he too had been pounded hard by yesterday's hail.

"Easy there, now," Fargo told the man, whose brown eyes were blinking at him. "We'll tend to you." Trying not to breathe too deep himself, he watched the man's labored breaths. The poor bastard was likely a goner anyway. If they'd happened by a day later, he'd be dinner for the buzzards. But Fargo knew he had to do whatever he could; there'd been a time or two when he'd been laid up in the middle of nowhere and some kind soul had helped him out. You couldn't repay obligations like that directly. You just had to help somebody when it was your turn.

Getting the shriveled man around to their side of the pond, so they could tend to him more comfortably, wouldn't be much of a problem, but Charlie might as well help. Fargo straightened from his crouch and started to call, but was interrupted by a horrified scream and then the unmistakable sound of retching.

"What the hell?" the Trailsman muttered. "I'll come fetch you in a minute, soon as I figure out what happened to my partner here."

Fargo stood straight and looked back. Curious Charlie hadn't stayed put. The kid had wandered back up that drag path, over a little rise. Not too far, because he could hear the kid puking up his guts.

The Trailsman's own stomach started churning as soon as he saw what Charlie'd found. Rotting corpses were bad enough, and those maggots that swirled in its sightless eyes did make it hard to keep breakfast down. But this body had been hacked at, too. Chunks of flesh had been sliced out of its thighs and shoulders. Its spread arms had been peeled almost to the bones that lay atop flayed and tattered skin.

Fargo got his arm across Charlie's lean shoulders and steadied the kid. "Disgusting as it is," he consoled, "this one's dead. We've got to tend to the living." He spun the kid toward the pond.

While they shouldered the survivor, who was too weak to walk, over to the grassy side of the pond, Fargo studied on the sign. There wasn't much to surmise, really. The living gent had been part of a party that ran out of food. Just how big that party had been back in Missouri was guesswork for now, but the group had dwindled down to two here, both too weak to travel well.

Then one cashed in, likely five or six days ago, right near some water. The other had been crawling back and forth, for as long as he could manage the short trip, from the water to the only food he could think of, his companion's raw and rotting flesh.

Time to turn Charlie into a nursemaid while the Trailsman dug out his sewing kit and hemmed up a pair of jeans for the short survivor. The man was so thin that nothing they had was going to fit him right. Meanwhile, Charlie grimaced and swabbed the sores. He mixed parched corn with water, into a thin gruel. The man didn't really have the strength to sit up and hold a cup, although he tried, so Charlie had to more or less pour it down his mouth.

This was as far as they were going to get today, dammit, so Fargo set up camp as Charlie continued to minister to their newfound cannibal. No, that wasn't fair, Fargo told himself. If a man knew where to look, he could generally find something edible most anywhere. But if this was somebody without much knowledge, you couldn't really blame him for not looking any farther than the corpse when his belly started growling fearsome.

"Bats. Get those bats away from me." The half-dead man's voice was cracked and hoarse, and he was trying to flail at whatever was attacking his face. All that was up there, though, was a terrified Charlie, who sprang back and looked over at Fargo.

"Shit," Fargo muttered, then answered the boy's question before he could ask it. "That happens sometimes when a gent's been through what this one has. They come unhinged and start seeing things that aren't there."

Now the man was trying to twist away from the big purple snakes he said he saw writhing around him. "Just leave him be, Charlie. You've done what you can do till he settles down."

"Mr. Fargo, what're we gonna do?" The quivering boy sank into the grass, almost atop the jeans Fargo had just hemmed up.

"Let's study on it. There's likely some wild turnips near this water, and I ought to be able to bring us down some meat for supper. But we can't stay here forever."

When Fargo said "meat," the kid started to choke, so the Trailsman continued. "Figure just the two of us, and we've got victuals enough for three or four days. We'd be riding, pushing at a fair clip, so we'd get into some better country by then. Can't be much more than a hundred miles."

"But with him?" Charlie still had trouble with a gagging throat as he pointed toward the man, who was now curled up because he was sure that some big boulders were rolling toward him.

"You're the one with the head for numbers, Charlie. You see what it might add up to."

Fargo stepped over to the victim, half-wondering if he ought to knock the gent cold so he'd quit writhing and muttering that awful stuff. But any bump might kill him, and besides, he was starting to calm down and just shake and shiver. The Trailsman spread a saddle blanket on the ground, rolled the man atop it, and threw another one over him. The sick man clutched the sweaty wool atop him and stared upward, as if he were an ant begging Fargo not to step on him.

"Think I got it figured out," Charlie glumly announced on Fargo's return. "I take it we had food for two people for four days and we could go thirty miles a day then. Now there's three, so that food's good for a little less'n three days. He won't be all that hungry, but he'll travel slow."

The boy took a deep shuddering breath and continued, "If we're going to tote that food, though, we'll still need the packhorse. But that gent ain't in any shape to walk. So one of us'll be taking shank's mare. Which gives us maybe fifteen miles a day, even if the going's good, and it ain't when we get much farther east, on account of godawful deep sand that pretty near stuck our wagons. Anyhow, we'd be lucky to get fifty miles afore we run out of food, and that's a long ways from anywheres."

Fargo hadn't figured it by the numbers, just by experience, but he knew the boy was right. "Sounds like the size of it, Charlie. You got any ideas?"

The boy shook his head. "Guess we just keep goin'."

They did, soon as the sun came up the next morning. Fargo walked, leading the Ovaro. Charlie generally walked with him, but sometimes sat lightly on the big pinto's saddle when he felt winded. Their patient sat listlessly atop the gelding, hardly ever speaking, like a man who really wasn't there. The roan went back to carrying the packsaddle. Tied at its rear was what remained of an antelope haunch after last night's dinner. At least something had gone right when Fargo had toted the Sharps up a rise just before sunset. With antelope, the first shot always had to be good, because the herd would spook and take off as soon as the noise reached their sensitive ears.

The haunch had lasted for three days of buffalo-chip fires at campsites that kept getting harder to find, because the thunderstorm residue had evaporated, leaving only the usual waterholes, which weren't exactly common. They were back to jerky and parched corn. As Charlie had predicted, recalling his previous trip across the Smoky Hell, the ground got worse.

Bizarre rock formations poked out of the prairie, extending twenty or thirty feet up into the scorching air. Clouds of choking dust swirled up with every step. The sandy soil swallowed a man's footsteps, making every stride the result of painful effort. Not even short brown buffalo grass grew out here. The plant life appeared to be confined to about fifty different kinds of cactus.

Most of it was low clumps of prickly pear, though. If he and Charlie had left all the spines in their hands, they'd have looked like porcupines. But they had to spend an hour or two at every camp, gathering prickly pear so they could roast the spines off and give the remaining fleshy part to the horses. Although they did try to graze, there was precious little else for them to eat.

The water they encountered kept tasting worse and worse, the farther east they got. Almost soapy, which meant the alkali concentration was rising. Sometime soon, they'd find water that crossed the line between distasteful and sickening, to where a man who drank it wouldn't do anything except shit his innards out for the next six or eight hours.

Charlie seemed to be taking all this in stride, maintaining his good nature. He even continued to pester hell out of Fargo with questions. And their companion had even started to take some interest in the visible world.

At times, he still tried to hide from the bats and giant snakes and wolves that he insisted were swarming all over the prairie, fixing to attack at any moment. But during his lucid moments, Fargo was able to learn enough to piece together the gent's story.

There'd been five of them at the start, back in Leavenworth, Kansas: Daniel Meyer, who rode with them now; his brothers, Alexander and Frank; and two others. They'd navigated by a story in the Leavenworth newspaper that sent them up the north fork of the Smoky Hell with assurances that they'd find ample game, grass, and water.

So they'd been hoofing it, with just a packhorse, as they passed the springs and the land got barren in a hurry. The packhorse took off one night, leaving them with precious little in the way of supplies or gear. The other two gents decided to go hunting, either for the packhorse or for something to eat. They'd been gone for four days when the Meyer brothers, almost out of food, decided to press on. Frank was the first to die, and after two foodless days, they swallowed their inhibitions along with some of Frank.

Alexander and Daniel struggled on westward, sure that all the gold they'd find in Colorado would more than make up for their travail. Gaunt and stumbling, his thirsty throat choked by dust, Alexander just lay down and told his brother to go on. Daniel wouldn't abandon him, and found that pool just over the rise. He took Alexander a few cupfuls, but he was dying. His last request was that Daniel use his body for food.

Such thoughts kept creeping into Fargo's mind, no matter how much he tried to dismiss them, every time he considered their situation. They'd be out of food by tomorrow, maybe the day after, even though he'd been running on short rations, figuring that beanpole Charlie and broomstick Daniel needed the food more. There hadn't been game worth mention out here, unless you counted a few birds that sometimes chirped from the sagebrush. Finding water was also getting to be chancy.

Living on prickly pear and scattered bunchgrass wasn't doing the horses a bit of good; they looked scraggly and moved grudgingly. The dappled gelding, Fargo decided, would be the first one that they'd butcher for food. Then the roan mare. And after that . . . Well, shit, he'd sooner slice up Daniel than his Ovaro. No, dammit, quit thinking that way. Just keep putting one foot in front of the other, even when you wobbled and slipped and sank in this godawful sand while the sun beat on you and you sweat away all that precious water you'd worked so hard to find.

The trail was starting to look like an extended junkheap. Every few yards, there was something that got tossed out of wagons back in the days of "Pikes Peak or Bust." After a week or so of plodding through this sandy desolation, folks decided they didn't really need grandfather clocks, ornate cast-iron stoves, hall trees, boxes of books, grandma's chinaware, sideboards and rocking chairs, and most other furniture. One pioneer had even discarded his Colt navy revolver, which had hardly rusted at all; Fargo cleaned it up and gave it to Charlie after a lesson that was too short because he didn't dare consume much of his stock of powder, balls, and caps. Every mile or so, a rough cross marked a trailside grave; too damn many of them belonged to children.

At least they were finally trending downhill, which made the going a little easier as they followed the ruts through the sagebrush. Good ruts. They held fresh wagon tracks.

Just who had been brave or stupid enough to come across here recently was a good question. Four or five ox-drawn wagons, from the look of it, and they couldn't be more than a day or two ahead. If they had been mindful about filling their water barrels, though, and carried enough supplies, they were likely managing okay.

If he could catch up to them, Fargo reckoned, they might have a chance of living through this. On horseback, catching up wouldn't be much of a problem, since ox teams didn't move any faster than you could walk. But his crew was lumbering along at the same maddeningly slow pace.

One more day, then. Fargo explained his plan to Charlie. "The Ovaro would have healed up total by now, if he'd been eating good. But he's still the best we've got, and tomorrow night, I'm going to climb aboard him and push his carcass just as hard as I can."

Charlie nodded. "Kind of wondered why you hadn't decided on that before, Mr. Fargo. Catching them wagons looks like our best shot. And I reckon I can stay back here and tend to Mr. Meyer, if'n you don't take too long."

"Glad to hear that, Charlie." The Trailsman told his stomach to quit gnawing at his backbone, and tried to concentrate on making one foot move ahead of the other.

10

As it turned out, they didn't have a bit of trouble catching the wagons. Early the next day, they crested a bleak rise, and not a quarter-mile ahead were four canvas-topped prairie schooners.

Trouble was, they weren't moving, except for the canvas flaps that fluttered in the morning breeze.

The Trailsman ignored the weariness that came from extended short rations and turned to the boy walking at his side. "Your tender stomach up to this one?"

Charlie swallowed hard and nodded. "But what about him?" He pointed at gaunt Daniel Meyer on the gelding. Meyer looked damn near as spooky as that horse sometimes did. If they left him there while they walked up and looked around, he just might bolt off. And if he came along and saw what promised to be some more sickening carnage among those wagons, he might get even crazier, just when it looked as though the man's bizarre visions were settling down to not much more than nightmares.

"Guess we'll do what you do with a horse," Fargo said, motioning Meyer down. Charlie held the man while Fargo tied hobbles, linking his ankles so that Meyer could neither mount a horse nor walk more than about a mile an hour. It was a rank way to treat somebody, but the Trailsman didn't see much choice.

Four men lay dead, sprawled in the square formed when the four wagons had drawn up abreast. They all sported typical bullwhacker garb, baggy twill trousers tucked into high-topped boots, frayed shirts, and dark long coats that hung almost knee-length. All they lacked was the low-crowned and wide-brimmed hats that ox-drivers favored, but it was understandable that they weren't wearing headgear, since each bearded man was scalped.

"Injuns?" Charlie asked as Fargo knelt and tried to ignore the stench as he examined the corpses.

"Maybe." There were arrow shafts protruding from these bodies, but Fargo wanted to be sure. He looked closer. Some of these men—no, make that all of them—had bullet wounds, too. And there was still plenty of congealed blood around the bullet holes, whereas the skin around the arrow shafts was virtually bloodless.

"Not Indians." Fargo rose and walked over to where Charlie was leaning against a wagon, shaking so much that he was sloshing the water in the barrels at its rear. Water. Before getting to Charlie, Fargo went the long way around and checked the barrels. Both were near full.

"They're scalped and they got arrows stickin' out of 'em. It's gotta be redskins," Charlie insisted.

"Somebody would like us to think that, Charlie. But that doesn't add up."

"Why not?"

"Well, let's think about it. Where we are, the only Indians likely to be about are Cheyenne and Arapaho. Sure, the Comanche and Kiowa come this far north from time to time, and it isn't unknown for the Dakota to swing south this far, and it could be that the Pawnee sometimes venture this far west. But we'd best look at what's most likely."

Fargo tugged the boy toward the nearest vacant-eyed corpse. "Look there. See how the scalp was peeled from the front? Arapaho don't always take scalps, but when they do, they start at the back, just above the neck."

"Cheyenne, then," the boy muttered, fighting with his strong impulse to look in some other direction.

"Look at the hands."

The boy stared along the arm, to hands that had last clutched a rifle in life; whoever had hit these wagons had ridden off with the guns. "Look normal to me."

"Right. That's why it isn't Cheyenne. All the other tribes that know the Cheyenne call them a name that means 'Those who cut fingers.' In sign language, you indicate the Cheyenne this way." Fargo held out one hand palm down and chopped at the base of the spread fingers with his other hand. "Whenever the Cheyenne count coup on an enemy, they don't just take his scalp. They always cut off some fingers."

Charlie stood silent and stared, then noticed what Fargo had earlier. "Look, Mr. Fargo. They got bullet holes and there's blood all around 'em. But there's hardly any at the arrows. Which means them arrows was stuck in after they was dead."

"Now you're learning how to read sign, Charlie." The kid brightened, but got glum again as Fargo continued, "Fetch that short shovel off the packhorse, and you and Daniel start digging a grave while I look around some more."

"Do we, do we have to, er, uh . . ." Charlie waved at the bodies and made pulling motions.

"Put a rope around them and drag them if you want to," Fargo said. "They're not going to mind. And if that gets to you, well, I'll help you out. But try to do it on your own, hear?"

Charlie nodded and walked back to the hobbled Meyer, then got the shovel.

As Fargo had half-suspected, this wagon train had been raided for such food as it might have been carrying. Crates were strewn all around, along with some empty tins. Those and the footprints showed that the raiders had been so damn hungry that they'd stopped to eat then and there, and just thinking about it made Fargo's empty stomach growl all the harder. He saw where they'd butchered one ox, then the trail left by the other dozen or so that were being driven off.

As if he needed further confirmation that the raiders hadn't been wearing war paint, those tracks that remained were those of shod horses, not the hooves of Indian ponies.

Fargo walked back to the wagons and looked inside. Three were pretty much empty, except for a little clutter, but the fourth held a trunk. When he slid it back from the wagon wall, he found a gunnysack half full of cracked oats, maybe fifty pounds.

Good. The damn horses would get fed while his

belly kept on growling. Well, no, they could share. Fargo stuck a handful of the dry grain in his mouth, strolled out to the remaining water barrels, where a dipper still hung inside one, and chewed hard for several minutes.

Charlie and Daniel waved from their work on a common grave. This ground was so sandy that they were already a yard down, and cussing plenty at the way the walls kept collapsing into the hole.

Pulling his belt knife, Fargo went back to the trunk. He slid the blade in the crack where the top came down atop the latch, and worried it some until the thing opened.

No food inside. Damn. Women's clothes. A woman? Where the hell was she, then? He'd examined the area close; there were only four bodies, and they were all men's. He pulled the clothing out of the trunk and found about a dozen books on the bottom.

He picked up one from the top, a thick blue-backed volume entitled *Modern Trigonometry*. Well, now he'd found some food for the horses and some food for Charlie's appetite for numbers, even if he hadn't found much to put under his own ribs. He was about to lay it back in the trunk, the best place for it under the circumstances, and then opened the cover.

Fargo's stomach quit growling. In fact, he was about to lose the oats he'd just put in it. "Simmer down," he told himself, "maybe you didn't read it right." He haltingly opened the cover again and looked at the title page. Right under the big printing with the book title, there it was in fine Spenserian script, good handwriting that was easy to read: "Property of Miss Florence Trefethen."

The other books were inscribed the same, and Fargo judged the clothes were about right for a lithe, willowy gal that was as tall as most men, about five-eight or so. He got serious about examining the interior of the wagon.

In a couple places, between the hoops and the canvas top, he found a few long strands of brown hair that had snagged when she'd been moving about inside. There was a dab of face powder on its rough wooden floor. Florence wouldn't have left without a struggle, Fargo was damn sure, but he couldn't find much sign of one. Maybe those fresh dents on the flooring and seat had come from her kicking heels, and then again, there wasn't any way to be sure just where they came from.

It was almost a certainty, though, that Florence Trefethen had arrived on her stagecoach in Denver about a week ahead of Fargo and Charlie. There she'd encountered some freighters who offered her quick passage to civilization. Bullwhackers could be plenty rowdy when they got to town, but they generally minded their manners toward any female passengers they might have. They took a professional pride in delivering their cargo undamaged, although they'd doubtless made sure she was aware that they were men and she was a woman.

Likely the cold-shouldered schoolmarm had managed to keep her distance from her traveling companions. Then two days ago, this train had been hit by hungry raiders. All four freighters had died in the struggle, and Florence, from the look of it, had been carried off to wherever they'd gone. To the south, judging by the tracks.

But they might as well have ridden straight up into the sky for all that Fargo could do about it. Shit. He was plumb out of stamina; every day it got harder and harder to keep walking. His belly was growling again, and he knew damn well those bedraggled horses needed those oats worse than he did. It'd take a week of grain and water before they'd be in any condition to tear off across this desolation in search of some prairie nighthawk crew.

Even if that were possible, by then the trail would be colder than a banker's heart, and Florence would likely be past needing rescue, anyway. Once the raiders had used her up, to where she quit bouncing under them while they took turns, they'd just kill her and leave her slender corpse to rot on the plains.

She'd been about as contrary as womenfolk ever got, which was plenty, Fargo mused. She'd had enough presence of mind to jab a robber in the balls, and then she'd managed to lose herself in some quivering sobs, totally unsure of herself. She'd taken every stitch of clothing off in front of a crowd of leering men, and yet she'd shown no interest in having any man warm her bed. She showed spunk and didn't back down from much of anybody, including the Trailsman.

Maybe that's why he felt so rotten when he dropped off the tailgate. If she'd just been among the bodies that the other two men were now covering, it'd be over. As it was, he knew she was getting abused fearsome, off in some owl-hoot camp that might be sixty miles away, and there wasn't a damn thing he could do except cuss about it.

He thought he would keep this to himself, but gave up on the notion when he got over to the grave.

Charlie handed the shovel to Daniel and looked the Trailsman over. "There's somethin' terrible wrong, ain't there, Mr. Fargo?" The kid, damn him, was getting real good at reading sign in people.

Fargo gave up on trying to keep a poker face. "Remember that schoolmarm up in Gouge-Eye?"

Charlie nodded, and Fargo proceeded to explain what he'd found. Meanwhile Daniel Meyer tried to decide whether it would be disrespectful to stomp around and pack the dirt down firmer on the grave.

At least they had some water here, and wagon parts made a much better fire than buffalo chips. They all had oatmeal porridge as the sun started to sink.

It was a good thing that Fargo had cooked up plenty of it. Just when they sat down and were eating comfortably, enjoying an abundance of water for a change, they had company.

From out of the shadows materialized two Cheyenne braves, clad in nothing but breechcloths. They didn't look all that starved, but they rubbed their bronzed, muscled abdomens in a way that you didn't need to know sign language to understand.

Their arrival was more of an annoyance than a surprise to the Trailsman. He figured that Indians had probably been shading them for the past week.

Fargo ladled some more porridge into the empty tins the two braves had picked up. They squatted;

instead of eating the stuff with spoons, they tipped the cans like cups and poured the stuff down. Whenever they weren't guzzling their chow, they glanced around warily with their round brown eyes.

Charlie sidled over next to the Trailsman. "What're we gonna do?"

"Stay as polite as we can be to our company, I reckon."

"Who are they?"

"Didn't introduce themselves yet. Cheyenne is all I can tell. I know a smatter of their language, and a lot of them have some of ours. And there's always sign language. So after dinner, maybe we'll jaw a spell."

"But they're wild Injuns, Mr. Fargo. They might just massacre us right where we stand."

"Charlie, those two bucks have likely been shading us for a week. If they meant us any harm, they'd have swept down on our camp some night. Depending on just how well I could shoot in the dark, they'd either be dead back there somewhere, and we'd have a whole proddy tribe out after us, or else they'd be adding our fingers to those necklaces they wear when they're in full war gear."

Charlie didn't seem to understand. "But ain't you gonna do somethin'?"

"Yes. Reckon I'll go over and introduce myself. You can come along if you can keep your mouth shut." He looked over at Daniel. The gaunt, silent man was like a horse; if there was food and water here, he wasn't about to light out for anywhere else, even if there were two Cheyenne warriors squatting only twenty feet away.

The Trailsman walked over to the Cheyenne braves and waited for them to finish draining their cans of gruel before greeting them in their own tongue.

They, in turn, explained that they were mighty grateful for the meal, but just had to move on right then. They both turned on their bare feet and headed out of the ring of light around the fire, into the vast over-whelming darkness. A minute later, Fargo heard their mounts stepping through the sand.

"What happened?" Charlie asked, obviously terrified that they'd done something to piss off the Cheyenne.

"Don't know. It's a new one on me," Fargo replied.
"Indians around camp are generally as chattersome as
magpies. Those boys didn't look all that surly, though.
They just ate and ran."

"We gonna have to stand guards tonight?" Charlie
asked.

Fargo couldn't see what good it would do. Exhausted
and feeling sick inside whenever he thought of food or
Florence, he wasn't in any shape to stay up all night.
He could trust his senses to rouse him if somebody did
invade their camp. Charlie wouldn't know what to do
on night guard duty, and he wasn't yet much of a hand
with that navy Colt. As for Daniel Meyer, he might
just start blasting away at bats or vultures or maybe
even flying buffalo.

But maybe this was like that stupid trick of laying a
rope around the bedrolls. It didn't keep snakes away,
but it made folks feel better, so they slept more comfortable. And if they weren't edgy and sitting up scared
shitless two or three times a night because they thought
they'd felt a snake when it was only their own arm
brushing against a leg, then everybody, even the non-
believers, got a better sleep.

"Okay," Fargo conceded. "No guns, though. You
see or hear somethin' suspicious, you rouse me." Both
nodded, and he crawled into his bedroll, lighter than
usual on account of the blankets he'd contributed to
making up a bed for Daniel Meyer.

Shit. He was stuck in the middle of dismal country
where a buzzard could die of starvation or thirst. Oats
or not, the haggard horses were going to give out
shortly; it was just a matter of time before one or
more would fall and refuse to get up. He still ached
from the hailstorm a week ago, and he hadn't eaten
anything properly describable as a meal for the best
part of that week. His traveling companions consisted
of a kid who still dripped behind the ears, and a
stumbling skeleton who was at least half-crazy; Charlie
wasn't bad company and Daniel managed to keep

pretty much to himself, but in any kind of jam, both would be more hindrance than help.

A woman that he couldn't help but worry about had been hauled off a wagon train by half a dozen shit-heel outlaws, and he couldn't do anything about it. Then two Cheyenne show up in camp, devouring what little food they had left and acting spooky the whole time.

It seemed to Fargo that he'd just quit pondering all that when he felt Meyer's bony, gnarled hand on his shoulder. Usually, he woke instantly, but the exhausted and hungry Trailsman had to blink away the grogginess as he peered into the darkness, able to discern only that rail-thin shape blotting out a few stars.

"What is it?" he finally grunted, keeping his voice down.

"Redskins."

"In camp?" Fargo pulled his pistol up from the blankets and sat up. There was a sliver of a moon, and the world began to take form.

"No. All around us, though."

Good. Maybe they'll just ride in and kill us all and put us out of our misery, Fargo thought. The Cheyenne were charitable that way. Whereas the Comanche and Sioux liked to torture their captives for days with slow fires and little flesh gouges from their stone knives, the Cheyenne simply killed any men they captured, generally braining them right then and there with war clubs. The women and kids got hauled off to join the tribe, and a surprising number of such white folks stayed Indian, even when they got a chance later to be ransomed or rescued.

But Fargo didn't mention those thoughts to Daniel Meyer. After pulling on his hat, he stood up in his balbriggans and joined Meyer in scanning the land that rose away from them.

The man's eyes must have been good, because it took Fargo twenty or thirty seconds to make out the first mounted brave, about a hundred yards off, in the direction opposite the setting moon. Once he saw the dim pattern, though, he didn't have any trouble seeing horses and their warriors every which way.

"Can you get them with your Sharps?"

The man's mind was a lot more than half gone if he thought that a man with a Sharps had any chance at all against what had to be better than forty warriors. No matter how fast and straight you shot, no matter how quickly you could jam powder and balls and caps into the gun, one brave would manage to get close enough, and that's all it would take.

"Suppose I could get a few," Fargo explained. "But it's really too damn dark for good shooting. Might as well wait till sunup and see what happens then."

"But they might attack then. They never attack at night," Meyer insisted.

"They sure might," Fargo said. "So we'd best rest up for it, right?" He patted Meyer on the shoulder and pointed the addled man to his bedroll. Charlie lay nearby, snoring a little.

When the sky finally got pink, about a century later, Fargo was up and dressed. The battalion of Cheyenne still perched out there. The only possible cover was the wagons, and they might manage to stand off the Indians for a day if they all had rifles and knew how to use them. But two pistols and a Sharps didn't add up to much against all that force out there.

Fargo studied more on heading for the wagons when three of the horsemen, all clad in the trailing eagle-feather headdresses that chiefs wore, started riding toward him. They raised their hands in the universal sign of peaceful intentions. Fargo holstered his Colt and waved back.

Even by this uncertain light, he recognized Black Kettle's distinctive features. The man was short and husky, with a hatchetlike nose and some bags above his cheeks that made his eyes look even rounder on his lined face.

Summoning such Cheyenne as he could muster after the chief alit and stood before him, the Trailsman told Black Kettle that his heart soared to greet his brothers and that his spirit was grateful that they were coming in peace.

"This person's heart is glad, too, that his brother, the Trailsman, still remembers the speech of a Real Person," Black Kettle responded. He introduced the two men with him, Dull Knife and Strong Nose. They, too, were chiefs, which wasn't quite the distinction among Cheyenne as in most other tribes, since the Cheyenne had forty-four men in attendance every time they summoned all their chiefs to a council meeting.

They palavered a bit before Black Kettle asked about Fargo's companions. Explaining them would take more Cheyenne than Fargo knew, and it would be tricky in sign language. But it wasn't as though he had much choice except to be civil, so Fargo started gesturing, explaining that Charlie was the son of a white chief, rich in useless gold rather than useful horses, who desired the Trailsman to escort the young man safely to a big school that sat a long ways off, over in the direction that the sun was rising.

Dull Knife spoke tolerable English that he'd picked up from traders and trappers, and the others seemed to understand enough not to need translation when he replied.

"My ears have heard and my eyes have seen that my brother the Trailsman is a good person that speaks in the ways of the Real Persons. He will please forgive me for speaking in the forked tongue of the Men Who Tell Lies so that he might feel more at ease."

Fargo nodded and said that English would be fine with him if it was okay with them. Then he started trying to explain what he was doing with Daniel Meyer. Dull Knife held up his hand. "We know about Man Who Eat Brothers. We had to kill two of his foolish brothers, who left their band, then began to shoot when they met some Real People who wanted to help them. Why is your kind so afraid of the Real People?"

Fargo could think of several dozen good reasons to feel edgy around Real People, but he figured the question was just part of the usual long-winded redskin rhetoric, and so he nodded sadly and let Dull Knife continue.

"The other three in the band. One dies and his brothers eat him. We found that butchering, followed trail. Figure maybe we help, or at least kill them before they hurt others. He eat other brother, too?"

Fargo nodded. "Back a spell. The man's still half-crazy, but he's coming around. More food would help. Fat cow would be a blessing, but the Great Spirit has sent none to our path."

The three Cheyenne smiled in commiseration. "But you still fed him when you had little food and set him on your horse while you walked in the dirt like a woman."

Well, if the Indians wanted to think he was a sissy for trying to do what's right, let them. He doubted he could get all three with his Colt before one got him, but he could sure as hell try if they pushed this much further.

The Indians changed the subject and pointed to the wagons. Fargo didn't mention the woman, and the three chiefs agreed the raiders were likely long gone. Then they jawed some about the whoa-haws and goddams.

When a Plains Indian said anything about a cow, he meant a buffalo. Oxen were whoa-haws because that's what the bullwhackers hollered at them all the time, and the first Indians to see wagon trains had just assumed that "whoa-haw" was what these strange animals were called. As for "goddams," those were bullwhackers, since that's what they hollered when they weren't saying whoa or haw.

Dull Knife returned his gaze to Fargo. "When my brothers came to your camp last night, you fed them."

Fargo nodded.

"When I visit the towns of the White Eyes, they want gold before they feed me or take me into their lodges. My lodge is always open and my food is always given to visitors. That is the way of the Real People."

Dull Knife put a hefty hand on Fargo's shoulder. "You, Trailsman, look like the White Eyes, but you fed my brothers and did not ask for gold. You fed Man Who Eat Brothers. You took him into your camp and into your journey. You wear stupid clothes and your skin is too pale, but your strong heart does not travel the crooked road of the White Eyes. You walk the straight path of the Real People. You and your brothers will ride with us to the camp of the Real People and the People of the Clouds."

11

Indians generally took their time at what they did, since they didn't use watches or even calendars, but the Cheyenne pounded hard as they moved east across the broken prairie. By the time the hot summer sun finally started slipping toward the featureless western horizon and their shadows grew long before them, Fargo figured that he, Charlie, Daniel, and the entire band had covered at least forty miles.

The Indian encampment sprawled for hundreds of yards along a bench above a fair-sized creek, one almost too big to jump across, and sat almost inside a considerable cottonwood grove. Those trees, visible for miles across the dusty plains, might have looked like a "smoky hill" to somebody once upon a time. Fargo figured that came as close as any other theory to explaining why the two creeks that joined nearby were called the Smoky Hill River.

As they dropped toward the Indian settlement, Charlie pulled up next to the Trailsman. "Why're there two camps down there?" He pointed to one semicircle of tepees, open to the east, like all their entry flaps. The other gathering sat more haphazard.

"The neater camp belongs to what the Cheyenne call the Cloud People. We call them the Arapaho. The other's the Cheyenne camp."

"That's a curiosity, Mr. Fargo. I thought them redskins fought each other all the time that they wasn't fightin' us."

Fargo sidled to get a little more comfortable atop the sassy paint that Dull Knife had lent him, and looked to be sure the unburdened Ovaro was still with them. "Lot of truth to that, Charlie, but the Cheyenne and Arapaho have been friends for a long time. They talk pretty much the same lingo—Cheyenne sounds a little harsher—but as best I know, they never bother to learn each other's talk. They use sign language between tribes, which seems kind of foolish, since they camp and hunt together so much. Cheyenne aren't quite as tall, in general, and they're a tad darker. But both tribes run tall and light for Indians."

"Do they dress the same?"

"Pretty much. You look at the beadwork, especially on the womenfolk, and where the Arapaho make white backgrounds, the Cheyenne will use tan beads."

"You sure know your Indians, Mr. Fargo." Charlie got a better grip on his own borrowed paint as they neared the twin villages. "There much other difference between 'em?"

"Sometimes it's life and death to know which tribe you're around," the Trailsman replied. "As for which tribe's which right ahead of us, they hang around each other's camps. Sometimes they ride together. Both groups stay pretty clean, especially for Indians. Hell, the Arapaho likely take baths more often than most white folks do; I've seen them break ice in a river just to clean up. A lot of Cheyenne talk English, and Arapaho don't. About the only other thing worth mentioning is that the Cheyenne raise their women fairly pure, whereas the Arapaho are pretty open-minded about what a gal might or might not do with the young braves before she marries."

Fargo realized he'd told young Charlie more than he ought to have, but he didn't know any way to take back his words. Any other such worries got lost in the tumult of their arrival.

There was only one nervous moment: when he met the Arapaho leader. Besides being the only southern Arapaho who spoke English, Niwot, or Left Hand, was their peace chief; he was a reasonable sort whom Fargo'd met a time or two before. But the gent who greeted him was Little Raven, the tribe's war chief. That didn't bode well, but then it turned out that Niwot and a few braves were out hunting some more fat cow, and they settled down to some serious feasting on roasted buffalo hump.

Then it was time to settle in for the night. Poor Daniel Meyer got wretched sick at the sight of the roasting meat. Then he started jabbering that big blue eagles were starting to swoop down and carry men off. A Cheyenne medicine man seemed to think that might be a prophetic vision worthy of study. He took Meyer over to his lodge.

Fargo and Charlie each got their own tepees, over on the Arapaho side. Doubtless it meant several families would be crowded that night, but that was the way of the Indians. When they were surly, nobody could be meaner; when they were hospitable, nobody gave more of whatever they had to their guests.

For the first time in a fortnight, the Trailsman's stomach wasn't growling. He started to settle into his bedroll atop a buffalo rug when the camp got noisy outside. He peeked out the tepee flap. Niwot's hunting band had just returned, their travois laden with humps and tongues and hides, which explained the commotion and why the fire had been rekindled.

The noise and the shifting patterns of light that played against the tepee wall might have been annoying if Fargo hadn't been so tired. But he didn't have any trouble ignoring such distractions as he sank back and felt himself pleasantly sinking into sleep.

In about a minute, he was almost ready to start snoring and dreaming, when the hairs at the back of his neck started to bristle. He forced his grudging eyes open and reached for his Colt. Surely the damn Indians hadn't feasted him and hosted him just to crawl into his lodge and brain him. But why the hell else was there that fluttering at the flaps?

Fargo dropped the Colt under the blankets and pulled the throwing knife out of his boot. The Colt worked better, but the knife was silent. He'd need silence if he were going to handle this stealthy attacker and then manage an escape. The flaps still showed that somebody was working in slow and stealthy, so he lay back, hoping to feign sleep and get the advantage of surprise.

But he lost that advantage when the attacker slipped

in, because he was the one that was more surprised. The dim and swaying light revealed an Arapaho gal in a beaded doeskin dress. Her hands were empty, and her face, framed by long locks that weren't braided, showed the hint of a smile.

Fargo sat up and signed, trying to be polite about it. "Why does this sister visit this person in the night?"

Her answer was in a gesture language that even whites in cities would understand. She just pulled off that doeskin skirt and stood there, bare-ass naked, her ripe brown breasts aquiver. The Trailsman's eyes moved to her slender, muscled waist, then the rounded shadows where her slim thighs came together. She didn't give him any more time for looking. Once she saw that he was watching, she just stepped on over to his bedroll and slithered inside.

Her fingers immediately began to rub his shoulders while his own hands traced down from her shoulder blades to the small of her back, then the swell of her heaving buttocks. Recalling that the Arapaho weren't fond of kissing, he nuzzled at her breasts as they got side to side while getting to know each other better.

She didn't believe in long introductions, though. Moments later, she'd rolled on her back and was pulling him atop her. Fargo forgot how sleepy he'd just felt and rolled over, landing between her upthrust thighs. Their strong sleekness enveloped him, pushing him toward where he was planning to go anyway. Her trembling moistness felt ready enough for his shaft as he entered.

Fargo felt overdue, but figured it was just common courtesy not to plunge in deeper until they'd warmed up a bit. Then his Arapaho bedmate thrust herself up toward his pelvis while her thighs demanded that he push himself into her. Glad to oblige, he saw her eyes grow wide for a moment as she stilled her writhing and the pressure of her internal tightness intensified.

She got used to the idea in about twenty seconds, though, and started bouncing like a bronc with a burr under its saddle. He had no trouble staying aboard, even when she started pounding hard on his back with clenched fists. Every so often, she hit one of the hail bruises that hadn't quite healed. So he slid his hands up from her buttocks and gripped her lean shoulders. That quieted her thrashing arms some. He pulled her excited body so that he was touching bottom on every feverish stroke.

Then he erupted, which made her even wilder, tossing and turning every which way. Once she had him, she wasn't about to let go. Fargo figured that after all that exhausting walking on short rations, he'd be finished for the night, but much to his surprise and their pleasure, he felt himself stirring again as he remained deep inside her.

For their second go-round, though, she sat atop him, doing most of the work, pounding and waving as her delectable breasts bounced in the muted but flickering light that seeped into the tepee. Fargo exploded with such vigor that he was sure he'd shoot her up through the smoke vent, twenty feet above him. But all that happened was that they finally settled down.

Still naked, she sat on his bedroll and started waving her hands. "This person is called Dancing Clouds," her gestures said. "Dull Knife says Trailsman follow path of Those Who Cut Fingers. Trailsman also follow path of the Human Beings." She had a big smile.

Well, if that's what it took to get along with the Arapaho, Fargo figured they'd manage just fine. From what she added, he got the idea that even though the Cheyenne thought he was an okay gent, the Arapaho were still suspicious. So Little Raven had asked her to find out whether the Trailsman comported himself in accordance with proper Arapaho etiquette. Sometimes that meant eating dog-meat stew in a smoke-filled tepee, and sometimes it meant being real friendly with the Arapaho women.

Dancing Clouds was still cuddled next to him when the Trailsman awoke, so late that the tepee wall glowed from direct sunshine. He patted her shoulder affectionately, pulled on his clothes, and stepped outside. A runner summoned him to Niwot.

The tall young chief leaned against a woven backrest in front of a tepee toward the back of the village, and motioned Fargo to join him.

"So we meet again, Trailsman. How did you come to the camp of the Human Beings and Those Who Cut Fingers?"

Glad that he could use English, Fargo explained. This time around, he provided more details, especially about the wagon train—that a woman he knew had been abducted, and that the white raiders had tried to make it look like an Indian attack.

"The White Eyes are not happy to tell lies with only their forked tongues anymore," Niwot mused sadly. "Now they try to tell lies with their knives and guns and stolen arrows." The chief sat back, eyes closed, and looked like he was dreaming for a couple of silent minutes.

Then he sprang up. "Hear me, Trailsman. They will pay. Prepare to travel before this sun starts to fall."

Realizing that Niwot meant noon by that, which wasn't too far off, Fargo got to his feet. By then, the long-legged chief had trotted to the center of the camp and was shouting orders in his melodious native tongue, apparently summoning the Cheyenne warriors and scouts, as well as his own, to a war council.

Fargo hadn't been invited to the council meeting, which was just as well, since it took him the better part of two hours to assemble his gear, make sure it was all working proper, discover that his Ovaro still wasn't in any shape for hard work, and check on Charlie. The outgoing boy had found half a dozen other boys his own age, and they were all laughing hard every time he tried loosing an arrow at an old barrel hoop they rolled across the ground. Over in the Cheyenne camp, Meyer was still jabbering nonsense, and his medicine man, wearing a pair of buffalo horns, was still impressed by Daniel's powers of prophecy.

They rode south, trending some to the west. Cheyenne scouts had seen the raiders' trail several days ago, but hadn't paid much mind to it. Fargo's tan mount was big for an Indian pony, but it had doubtless been birthed on some spread in Texas, and then stolen by the Comanche, and then by one of these tribes.

Behind them thundered a small herd, close to two dozen horses, kept together and moving by two Cheyenne boys going out on their first war party. The idea was to ride fast and hard, changing mounts often, and perhaps stealing new ones if that became possible or necessary.

Up in front, the Trailsman rode with two Arapaho: Little Raven, the war chief, and Heap of Whips, a surly young buck who didn't much like Fargo but hated other White Eyes even more. With them were three Cheyenne chieftains, also in war paint and full battle regalia: Dull Knife, Tall Horse, and Spotted Wolf.

They were raising a huge cloud of dust, which perturbed Fargo some at first. But who the hell was going to bother them? He was with the local Indians, and nothing much smaller than a full cavalry troop of experienced men would stand much of a chance against them. He was riding with a picked group of elite warriors, the best that two prairie nations could muster. And they were riding hard, through the day, into the night, stopping only to swap or water their mounts.

Realizing that he'd been asleep in the saddle, the Trailsman shook himself awake as he sensed that their furious pace had slowed to a walk. It was late in the day and Dull Knife now rode next to him.

"Trailsman, the evil camp is near."

Fargo looked for landmarks, but all he saw was dust and choppy prairie. "We must be getting close to the Arkansas," he mused aloud. "You're sure you found their trail?"

Dull Knife spat and stared at him like he was an idiot. "It is theirs, Trailsman. The Big Timbers are no more than twenty of your miles. The evil men are between here and there. We attack at dawn."

Now they were starting to move slow and sneaky, so as not to alert anyone down along the mountain branch of the Santa Fe Trail that a war party was coming. When they reined up for a dry camp at sunset, Fargo talked matters over with Dull Knife.

Indians tended to just charge in on a raid like this. They liked to fight, and they were sure good at it, but they fought for the glory of it. They thought it was most important to count coup by touching the fallen enemy. If Florence was still alive down there, she could sure get killed—or take her own life, rather than be carried off by the savages—in the commotion that such a raid would provoke.

Fargo knew he didn't have much standing with this band of warriors. Weary as he'd been, it was about all he could do to stay atop his mount during this hard trip while the Indians looked for sign and handled the other chores.

Nonetheless, he chomped on some pemmican and explained his plan to Dull Knife.

"It is not the usual way of the Real People and the Cloud People," the chieftain replied before using the last of the daylight to explain the Trailsman's proposal in sign language.

Heap of Whips liked the notion, though. He said the only thing the White Eyes were good at was trickery and slaughter. It was only sensible for the Human Beings and Those Who Cut Fingers to learn as much of that as they could. Then they could better defeat the invaders who grew more numerous every year.

Fargo didn't feel real comfortable teaching Indians any new ways to pester white folks. But what the hell. These gents had fed and sheltered him and two fairly helpless people. They hadn't sent a posse after him. Maybe they raided wagon trains that crossed their hunting grounds every now and again, but they hadn't raided the one he was concerned about.

Not long after the sun peeked over the east rim of the earth, the Trailsman stepped toward a dugout soddy. Bigger than most, it backed into a hillside about ten miles north of the Arkansas River. A nearby seep provided water for what had to be at least five people inside, judging by the tracks and the horses hobbled in a low spot. Some of those tracks showed fresh evidence of a bare foot, shorter and leaner than the boot prints, so there was reason for hoping that Florence was still about. Of course, this might be some other outlaw hideaway, but the Trailsman figured that if you couldn't trust the Cheyenne to find the right trail, whom could you trust?

The idea was to draw as many men as possible

outside, without letting the woman inside see or hear him.

From fifty yards away, the Trailsman hollered. "Hello, the house." He knew somebody was up and about, because a few wisps of smoke were climbing out of the rusty stovepipe.

Nothing happened, so he stepped closer and hollered some more. Finally a bowlegged chunk of riffraff swung the plank door and peered out, one hand holding a shotgun.

"What's your problem?"

"This'd be the station house, wouldn't it?"

"What?"

Fargo made himself sound as stupid as possible. "The guidebook. It said there'd be a way station along here if we was to follow that new shortcut road, up from Big Timbers, over to Cherry Creek. Got me a busted wagon wheel about a mile back . . ."

"This ain't no station house, pilgrim. And that guidebook's full of shit. Never heard of no such road. Best you head back to the Arkansas if you know what's good for you." He started to slam the door shut.

"Guess I'll just have to find somebody else that'll help me get them womenfolk to Denver." The Trailsman turned and the shotgun man stepped on out the door, shutting it behind him as he shuffled toward Fargo.

"Now, wait a minute, mister. I think we can help you out here." His near-toothless mouth started to leer in anticipation of getting a few more women to be passed around back inside. But he didn't get to think much about it, because Little Raven, although lying prone on the dirt roof, still had good aim with a war club. The heavy stone end thudded against the back of the man's head, and he collapsed in silence. Fargo dragged the lifeless body out a few steps, hoping that Little Raven remembered when counting coup that the Trailsman didn't count.

It wasn't long before two gents stepped out the door, no doubt headed for morning chores with the horses, or maybe at the sagging privy. They saw their prone companion and looked up to see Fargo standing over the body.

"Hey, asshole," one shouted, reaching for his gun, "what'd you do to our buddy?" He caught Dull Knife's arrow, shot from inside a sage clump where you wouldn't think anybody could be hiding.

His companion whirled, saw the feathered shaft and the blood running down his friend's shoulder. He started to drop flat. He seemed familiar, and when Fargo saw the man's dirt-etched and astonished face, he recognized one of the would-be rapists he'd tied up way back when in Gouge-Eye.

Unperturbed by a couple of war whoops in the background, Fargo stepped forward and tapped the man's head with his boot. "You finally managed it, didn't you?" he grunted. "That schoolmarm still inside?"

The man seemed to be nodding as the Trailsman broke a couple of his ribs, and the son of a bitch started making strange noises behind him as Fargo walked toward the cabin door. Tall Horse was trying to be civil, slitting the men's throats before hacking off their fingers, but there was still a lot of horrified gasping and gurgling.

Now that there was a commotion in the yard, another man, dressed only in his balbriggans, got curious and looked out the door. "Injuns," he hollered. He might have lived a few minutes longer if he'd had the sense to duck back immediately, but he couldn't help looking at the bodies and dripping fingers that Tall Horse was waving at the sun. Or maybe it was the sight of the Trailsman, a white man stepping slow and deliberately toward the door, no more than ten yards off.

Maybe he saw Spotted Wolf materialize out of a dirt pile. He might even have seen the lance coming that pierced his heart, sending a fountain of fresh blood to splash across the door before he fell back.

Colt in hand, the Trailsman stepped on over the corpse and pushed the gory door open.

Against the back wall, a black-bearded man held Florence before him, with a dragoon pistol against her ear.

There wasn't much chance of her using a hat pin this time, since she wasn't wearing a hat or anything else. Her long hair looked stringy and dirty, protruding at bizarre angles in the dim light. Beneath her small and bruised breasts, her ribs showed, and she quivered like a wounded animal. A week or so of hard use had taken the fight out of her, and if she planned to say anything about it, she couldn't, since she was gagged. The man holding her obviously meant to use her body as a shield, or maybe to bargain with, as the situation demanded.

" 'Morning, Miss Trefethen," Fargo said.

"One step closer, mister, and I blow her head off."

"Guess I'll just stand right here, then."

"You some renegade half-breed, runnin' with them redskins?"

Fargo shrugged. "Well, actually I'm just a quarter-breed, and that's Cherokee. I'm not kin to the people in these parts."

"Just put that gun back in your holster, easy, you fuckin' renegade, afore I shoots this bitch. Her pussy's 'bout wore out anyway."

"It's your gun and your game," Fargo answered easily, "so I guess we play by your rules." He holstered the Colt.

His husky antagonist grinned, even as a few particles of dirt fell from the mud-and-pole ceiling. Heap of Whips had been digging real quiet up there. Now that there was a gap big enough for the slender brave to slip through, he covered it with a blanket to prevent daylight from entering and alerting the man right under him.

Having an opponent right against the back wall, right where the Arapaho warrior would enter from above, hadn't been part of the plan, but Heap of Whips knew how to adjust.

Still holding Florence before him, the burly man turned the Colt toward Fargo. "Now, you shit head, I'm going to teach you not to disrupt my pleasure."

Fargo's lake-blue eyes flitted up, as if he were trying to make connections for a final prayer. "You surely don't mean to kill me, mister, do you? I haven't done anything to you."

"Don't matter none, now, does it? You and your murdersome Injun buddies—"

He might have had more to say, but nobody ever got to hear it. Leaning down from his perch while he had his knees hooked across a pole, Heap of Whips swung the war club with surprising force for a lithe man with such slender arms. The power he put into that stroke would have shamed a lot of blacksmiths with brawny arms that swung heavy hammers all day.

The stone tip plunged into the man's ear, sinking clear to the rawhide that laced the handle on. Propelled by the blood of a smashed artery, hair and chunks of flesh sprayed out, some splashing on Florence's trembling shoulders. The man's eyes began to grow dull in silence. His smashed head lurched against a shoulder and he stayed put for a bit, propped up by the wall, then fell sideways to the dirt floor.

Fargo motioned to the smiling and upside-down Heap of Whips. "That is all of the evil men," he gestured in sign language. "This battle is finished."

Heap of Whips sent off a bloodcurdling whoop before landing on the floor, brandishing a scalping knife.

Even with her gag off, Florence just stood there in silence, still as a statue, while the Trailsman ignored the dugout's stench and searched among the rough bunks and general clutter for some clothes for her. Such female clothes as he found were much too short, so she wasn't the first woman these men had hauled in as a plaything. The calico smock he finally threw over her was supposed to extend to the ankles, but it barely covered her knees.

Once they got outside, he really couldn't blame her for not joining the general celebration of coup-counting, scalp-taking, and finger-chopping. But did she have to just stand there, staring glaze-eyed and never saying a word, not even when they hauled what remained of the bodies inside the soddy and caved in its roof? At least the Indians were good company, bragging on the fresh scalps and the new additions to their herd of captured horses.

Three days later, after a somewhat more leisurely ride back to the Smoky Hill camp, she still hadn't much more than hissed and pointed whenever she had something to say, which wasn't often.

Charlie, though, was as talkative as ever. When Fargo had arrived, the kid had a pile of arrows he'd won, playing a game where they rolled around a carved-up bone and bet on the outcome. He was getting to be a tolerable shot with the short bow they'd given him. If it hadn't been for his blond hair, he'd be hard to spot in the crowd of youngsters he was sporting with, since he'd taken to wearing a breechcloth and leggings during Fargo's absence.

Florence Trefethen, cold-shouldered as ever and now virtually silent, might need some more rest, maybe for the remainder of her life. But the Ovaro had recovered, and Fargo knew it was time to push on when Dancing Clouds sidled up to him. She indicated that she and several friends had visited the lodge of the yellow-haired brave. He, too, was becoming a proficient follower of the Way of the Cloud People, or at least the way some of their women liked to be pleasured under the blankets at night.

You couldn't ask for much nicer hosts, Fargo mused. Why, even Daniel Meyer, mere skin and bones a few days ago, was starting to flesh out, and he attracted an audience some nights while the medicine man translated his visions.

But the only reason Darius Hamilton hadn't chosen to send his son east by means of the stagecoach was because he thought an unsupervised boy might be lured by various corruptions. He was right, too. As Fargo watched, he realized that the half-naked blond warrior, now haggling over his winnings, had taken to gaming and women as thoroughly as he had to opium.

And the Trailsman had given his word that he'd get Charlie to school in St. Louis without picking up too many wayward habits. If they didn't get out of here shortly, the boy's morals would be beyond redemption.

12

They left Daniel Meyer with the Cheyenne and headed east. Another week there, and Charlie, too, would have wanted to ride forever with the Real People and the Cloud People.

After they passed the junction of the north and south forks of the Smoky Hill River, the going got easier. Maybe that was just by comparison, since the ground remained rough for a spell and western Kansas was still gray and parched from a drought that had started last summer and showed no signs of letting up.

The Trailsman, the boy, and the schoolmarm took three weeks to cross Kansas along the Smoky Hell Trail. Fargo didn't have to shoot more than a dozen hungry wolves. The only two prairie fires they spotted were too distant to be a bother. No sky-blackening plagues of locusts descended on them. Best of all, they'd somehow managed to avoid getting caught up in all the shooting and looting between the Jayhawkers and the border ruffians.

During the first few days of their resumed journey, Charlie was unusually tight-mouthed. He looked shame-faced, sure that Fargo was going to tan his hide for doing what came natural back in the Arapaho camp.

Finally they had a little talk. The Trailsman explained that he wasn't the boy's Sunday-school teacher, that if you're living with the Arapaho, you'd best act accordingly. The kid's good nature returned almost instantly; he was as curious and talkative as always.

It was Florence who was worrisome. She stayed at Fargo's side, and that kind of travel with a woman generally offered certain pleasures. He knew he could have shared a bedroll with her any night, but why bother? It would have been like bedding a corpse. She seldom said anything, and when she did, she mumbled only a few words. When she ate, she had to force in every bite and swallow. Florence Trefethen was just going through the motions of living.

Maybe she needed to talk this out with another woman, someone she knew well. Perhaps some of her kinfolk could tend to her until she recovered some interest in life. It could be that the once-feisty woman would remain sullen and withdrawn for the rest of her days; that sometimes happened. But Fargo didn't see any way he could help, besides making sure she arrived safely in St. Louis.

They'd be on their way now in a few minutes, as soon as their steamboat pulled out of Kansas City and started puffing down the Missouri River.

The low-pitched whistle echoed off the waterfront buildings, and the gangplanks started coming up Although the sun would set in less than an hour, and the calendar was nearing the end of August, the heat was intense and stifling. Ignoring Charlie's brisk chatter and Florence's brooding silence, the Trailsman stood on the promenade deck, scanned the lower deck, jammed with people and cargo, and cursed to himself.

That's where he and Charlie would spend the next two nights, more or less camped out in a crowd. Upon their arrival in Kansas City, Fargo had stabled the Ovaro and sold the other horses. After all that time in the saddle, he figured on splurging for some luxury on the last leg of this trip. But when he'd tried to book cabin passage, only one room was left. He reserved it for Florence.

Now that the gangplanks were up, the captain tooted the whistle again, and the paddle wheel started to churn the muddy water. Charlie spouted questions about boilers and engines, which Fargo tried to answer. After half an hour, a passing crewman overheard them and offered to take the inquisitive boy down to the engine room and show him around.

"Would you escort me to my cabin, Mr. Fargo?"

Fargo turned, just to be sure the words were coming

from Florence. That was the longest sentence she'd uttered since he'd found her in the outlaw dugout.

"Be proud to, Miss Trefethen. Sure you don't want to wait a bit, though? They'll be serving dinner any minute in the dining room downstairs."

"I'm not hungry, Mr. Fargo."

He shrugged and offered his arm. They shuffled slowly through the crowd to her room on the other side of the boat. At the door, she pressed the key into Fargo's hand, and he opened it. Her luggage—one trunk of new clothes he'd practically had to force her to buy this morning in Kansas City, with his money, at that—had been stowed in the room, so he didn't see that he was needed anymore. And besides, after that week of hungry walking, he wasn't going to miss any meals if he could help it.

She stood just inside the door, as mute and still as a marble statue, as Fargo started to step out after looking around the room.

The first sob came when he was right next to her, along with tears that were the start of a cascade that poured out of her gray and bloodshot eyes. "Skye, Skye, Skye," she gasped, her low voice choking with every word. Since the lithe schoolmarm was leaning his way anyway, fixing to collapse any second, he grasped her shoulders and steadied her.

That didn't stop her from burying her face in his chest as she continued to weep and tremble. "Skye, I've been so awful and you've been so kind. How will I ever repay you?"

"Easy now, Florence," he consoled, waltzing her in a step or two and maneuvering the door shut with his trailing foot. "You don't owe me anything."

Her arms found his waist, so that she could pull herself even closer. He patted the center part of her shoulder-length brown hair while her smothered words came out. "But—but it's your livelihood, getting people from one place to another. You told me that yourself. And I have nothing to pay you with, nothing at all." She shuddered all over, and he felt his shirt moisten with her tears.

"Florence, maybe the only reason I'm alive right

now and able to help you is because I don't insist that every customer be a paying customer." He hoped that would lighten her up a bit, but if it did, he sure couldn't notice. She just kept up her sobbing and clutching while he repeated Dull Knife's speech about the ways of the Real People.

"Sometimes you just have to do what feels right, even if it seems kind of foolish when you've got precious little food, and you still share it with two Cheyenne," he continued, explaining that that was why the Indians had taken them in, rather than leave them to grub about on the dry prairie with three famished horses.

As she replied, Fargo couldn't help but enjoy the way her small but firm and uncorseted breasts were rubbing against him. He silently told his own swelling desire to simmer down, but when he tried to step back, she just moved right with him.

"That's a cruel world out there on the Great Plains," he told her, "where people play rough and play for keeps. Those bastards who took you tried to make that wagon-train raid look like an Indian job. The Cheyenne and Arapaho can't imagine why you'd raid a wagon train and steal a woman, and not be bragging on it. The way the Indians see things, it's evil not to be proud when you've pulled off a coup like that."

"So that's why you all came to rescue me?" She stepped back, bristling with a spark in her eyes and some timbre in her voice. "Because your Indian friends were angry about some sort of evil in general?"

"That's likely why the five warriors rode out. But that's not why I did."

"Why, then, why? Another day or two, or even a week. I'd be dead by now. It would be over. I wouldn't have to live with that . . . those . . ." She started shuddering again. Fargo sat her down on the bed but remained standing himself.

She pulled her face out of her hands and wrung them before her as she looked up at the Trailsman. "I don't know, I just don't know. I love to teach, I really do. But I'll never get another teaching position. Never, ever. Those school boards, they watch you every minute anyway. You men can carry on all they want, but God help a single schoolmarm that so much as goes for a carriage ride with a man."

Fargo didn't know what to say, so he just sat down on the chair and nodded, so that she'd go on, maybe talk this out. The cabin was damn near dark now, but she leaned over and lit the lamp that hung on the wall.

"And now," she continued, her voice rising so that Fargo was glad the folks on the other side of the thin cabin walls were likely downstairs chowing down, "now I have the most awful reputation, I know. I lost control in Gouge-Eye, just let myself get carried away. Then, when I really got carried away, passed from man to man in that awful dirt dugout . . . Oh, God, I know everybody's staring at me and clucking, and they'll do that wherever I go, whatever I do."

"Florence, quit thinking you're so damned important."

"What?" she spat.

"Most people have more to do than worry about you and whether you've got a lurid past. If men eye you on the street, it's because you're a handsome woman, not because they're trying to remind you of what you did that they don't even know about. You're smart and you've got a lot of spunk and some damn day you'll figure out that you can do pretty much whatever you've a mind to do, no matter what's happened to you before. You're still walking and breathing, and I'd like to think it's just a matter of time before you start thinking again."

Almost in counterpoint to the way Fargo slumped back into the straight-backed wooden chair, wishing he was somewhere else, she got to her feet and stood directly before him. "Do you really mean that, Skye?"

Before he could even nod, she started unbuttoning her shirtwaist. "Then I'm going to do what I've a mind to do. Take off every stitch of clothes in front of a big, handsome man." The blouse fell and she started tugging at her skirt. "Then I'm going to roll back on that bed and spread my limbs wide while I watch him, the gallant knight that rescues damsels in distress, take off every bit of his clothes."

The skirt fell and she pulled the chemise over her

shoulders. Her breasts quivered almost in Fargo's face, the erect nipples aimed at his forehead. "Then I'm going to find out what it's like to swive when you're doing it because it's what you want to do, not because you'll get choked or shot if you don't."

Florence turned abruptly and sat on the bed, thighs spread. Before she rolled back to prop her head on the pillow, she had more to say. "Skye, I want to do what seems right."

What seemed right was for the Trailsman to peel off his clothes, although it felt a bit peculiar to have a naked schoolmarm gasp and giggle every time something came off. Fargo joined Florence on the bed, cuddling her, figuring that he'd best be gentle after what she'd been through.

"No, no," she protested as he nuzzled her breasts and massaged her cleft, starting slow. "Now. Not your silly finger. You. Your cock. The real thing. I want it, I want it all."

Seeing no reason to argue, Fargo plunged in deep as Florence arched her back and raised her slender hips to get all she could. He grabbed the feather pillow and slid it under her taut but vibrant rear.

That freed her legs for other important tasks, like wrapping him in a crushing scissors grip when she wasn't trying to dance across the ceiling. The Trailsman stroked slow and easy, like the rods that drove the big paddle wheel somewhere out there. But she had different notions, so their pace got frenzied. They pounded against each other.

It was hard to say who felt more pleased when they both exploded together in a furious mutual wave of ecstasy. And even while they caught their breath, she stayed wrapped around him.

"Oh, Skye, is this how it's supposed to be? It's so, so wonderful, you here against me and inside me and everywhere," she murmured, her head pressed against his scarred shoulder.

"I reckon so," he finally answered, enjoying the way the lamplight played on her expressive face.

She started to stir again and he felt himself stiffening, deep inside her. "Mmmmm," she moaned. "Think you could manage another lesson for a schoolmarm's continued education?"

Fargo managed. He managed so well that they didn't leave the cabin until the boat docked in St. Louis. Florence doubtlessly occasioned shameful gossip among the stewards, seeing as they ordered meals sent to the room, and Fargo tipped one cabin boy extra to keep an eye on Charlie and to summon him if the boy got in a jam.

Out on the teeming deck as the passengers swarmed to go ashore, Fargo caught up to curious Charlie. He quickly learned that the boy had talked his way all around the boat, from the engine room clear up to the texas. The captain had even let the boy toot the whistle and handle the wheel for a few minutes along a quiet stretch, a rare privilege.

The kid didn't seem to mind that he'd been neglected. He grinned at the sight of Fargo and Florence, and announced, "Mr. Fargo, I've made me a new friend. Lives right here in St. Louis, so I can see . . ." He turned, because his new friend was approaching through the throng on the deck. "Mr. Fargo, I'd like you to meet Danielle DeLyon."

"Oh, Jesus," Fargo muttered as Danielle bustled up, dazing him in a cloud of French perfume.

"Ooh la la." The woman laughed. Rolling her eyes, she laid a familiar hand on Charlie's chest. "*Mon ami*, you not say you travel with Skye Fargo. Skye and me old friends."

Fargo stared. Even if she was thirty-five or so, Dandy was still a pretty little thing. Black kohl emphasized the teasing light in her blue eyes. Rouge heightened the enthusiastic flush in her cheeks. A froth of lace spilled from the neckline of her trim, striped satin traveling suit. Her long skirts rustled as she bobbed forward to plant a kiss on Fargo's cheek.

"It's a pleasure to see you, Dandy," Fargo lied. Under different circumstances, that would be true. But the woman was trouble. She liked trouble.

"Skye," Florence murmured, her grip tightening, "do you know this woman?"

"Yep." Fargo nodded as he eyed the blond minx

known as Dandelion in St. Louis. How had Charlie ever found her? Not that she was difficult to find. She'd been known as Rosa Carmina in San Francisco—probably because her hair had been red then, and her accent Spanish. She'd been Two Hearts Terry in Virginia City, where she'd dealt cards in a gambling palace until they'd run her out for cheating. Sassy Sue in El Paso. Madame Dandy DeVine in New Orleans.

Fargo shook his head, trying to dispel the notion that he had totally failed at his job. While he'd been snuggling in a cabin with Florence, Charlie had found something a lot more potent than whiskey, more addictive than opium, and more fetching than the Arapaho girls. It was silly to think that way, Fargo told himself. After all, if just meeting up with Dandy was so dangerous, half the men in the West would be dead.

"Mr. Fargo, Miss DeLyon has offered me a job," Charlie blurted.

"What?"

"As her bookkeeper," Charlie added hastily. "And it will be wonderful. A real experience, Mr. Fargo. You can't beat real experience, now, can you? My pa, he had to work a long time to get where he is," Charlie babbled. "I'd be doing real work. Getting paid, too. Not many get an opportunity to learn business close up when they're as young as me."

"Charlie," Fargo growled, "I don't think your father would like this particular business."

The crowd on the deck milled past the tight foursome. Men stared at the two women. One young rogue winked knowingly at Dandy.

"But it'll just be till the school term starts," Charlie pleaded, noting Fargo's scowl. "As soon as the term starts, I'll hie myself right on over to that Covenant place."

"*Ah, oui*," Dandy asserted. "I will see to it myself. And zee boy is so talented. So good with zee numbers. So good with everything."

The woman was taunting Fargo. She tossed her blond curls back, offering a brilliant smile. Mischief danced in her eyes, and he remembered a few times that he hadn't minded her teasing. But this was different. Fargo glared at Dandy.

And Florence tightened her grip; her nails cut into his shirt. "Skye, I cannot believe that you are keeping me here in the presence of this false hussy."

"I'm not keeping you," Fargo muttered, shaking her fingers loose. "Besides, only the French is false. The hussy's real enough." He looked up. "Charlie," Fargo boomed, reaching out and spinning the boy away from Danielle DeLyon, "we are going to have a talk."

The boy read Fargo's intent. "If you can have fun, so can I," he hissed. Charlie spun and almost jumped several yards to Danielle's side.

Fargo turned to make sure he wasn't losing Florence in this crowd, which was getting serious about pushing and elbowing, now that the gangplanks had been dropped. He spotted her, rushing away, sobbing as she pushed through the mob of passengers. "Aw, shit," Fargo muttered, hurrying after her.

But what the hell. Once on shore, Fargo could find Charlie in a few minutes and get him to the Covenant Academy, even if he had to cold-cock the little whelp and drag him out there.

Fargo caught up with Florence. He grabbed her arm and she glared at him before jerking her head in the other direction so emphatically that it was a wonder her neck didn't snap. She neither looked nor spoke to the Trailsman as he scouted out a ride.

First Street in St. Louis ran right along the river. On this late-summer morning, it hadn't changed much since the last time Fargo had been through. Same row of gin mills, dance halls, card rooms, billiard parlors, fleabag hotels, and the like, although there was a new attraction. The soap peddlers must have been run out of Denver, because the same bearded gent was running his spiel here, along the waterfront.

Recalling why he generally avoided cities and their jostling crowds, Fargo got himself and Florence aboard a hack, bound for one of the better hotels several blocks away.

Florence settled on the cushioned seat across from

Fargo. Tugging and smoothing her skirts, she looked as bristling and mad as a wet hen. Suddenly, she was no longer quiet.

"I can't believe the way you've treated me," she hissed.

"Me?" Fargo snapped. "What did I do?"

"You dare ask? You, who leaves me, a school-teacher, standing on the deck with a painted-on, primped-up, rigged-out whore? Everyone was looking at us. The men were positively leering. Because that's what she was, you know," Florence spat, poking a finger at Fargo's chest. "She's a whore."

"I knew that," Fargo admitted quietly.

"And yet you left me with her anyway," Florence accused indignantly.

"I didn't leave you with her," Fargo objected. "Although if I had it to do over again, I just might."

"Why, you . . . you . . . You're as bad as Julius Houghton."

"Julius Houghton? Who in hell is Julius Houghton?"

"The chairman of the school board in Three Rivers, Iowa, that's who," Florence fumed. "And my fiancé. At least he was my fiancé until I found out he spent every Friday night in a brothel. That's why I had to go west. And now look what he's done to me," she wailed. "Everything's gone wrong. But you don't care, do you? You're not going to do a thing about it."

Fargo gawked at her. "Just what in hell do you expect me to do? I'm supposed to be looking after a boy who is right now getting into God knows what kind of trouble, and instead of doing my job, here I am escorting you to a hotel. But you don't appreciate that at all, do you?"

"Oh," she cried, flinging herself down on the seat. "Women like that Miss DeLyon get paid, but I'm supposed to appreciate it."

Fargo gaped. "Florence, that's not what I meant. You know that's not what I meant," he said, putting a hand on her shaking shoulder. "I guess maybe I said the wrong thing, but I'm a little worried about Charlie right now."

Florence shrugged away from Fargo's hand. "Men,"

she whimpered. "They always expect you to care about their work, but they never care about your life."

"That's not fair," Fargo chafed. "I saved your life."

"A lot of good it will do me," she moaned. "Julius will never take me back now. And I miss him," she sniffled. "Julius is a little boring, but he's comfortable. And how am I going to live without a man after the things I've learned? I just want to go home, and now I can't. Not after what I've done. Men can do anything they want. But women? Women can't do anything."

"Is that what you're worried about?" Fargo asked, handing her a handkerchief. "Hell, Florence, if Houghton's in Iowa, he'll never know the difference."

"I can't lie," she sniffed. "Besides, I'm a lot more experienced now. He'll know."

"I've got it," Fargo suggested. "Tell him you were taken by Indians. That's true, in a way. Tell him you can't bear to talk about it. And then weep a lot. It'll all work out."

"But that's dishonest."

Fargo shrugged. "This Houghton fellow, did he tell you about the brothel?"

"Of course not, I saw—"

"That's what I figured," Fargo interrupted. "I guess the two of you will just have to learn to be honest in the future. No sense worrying about the past."

The hack stopped. "Florence, we're at the hotel," Fargo said gently as the driver flung open the door. "You'll understand if I don't come in right now? I've got to find Charlie."

Florence glanced at the open door and then back at Fargo before she threw herself against his chest. She wrapped her arms around his neck. "Maybe it would be better if I don't see you again," she whispered.

"Whatever you think," he agreed.

"Do you really think Julius would take me back?"

Fargo put his hands on her shoulders and pushed her back to where he could see her face. "Certainly," he said, nodding as he looked into her shining eyes. "He'll take you back."

Florence smiled, and Fargo knew for certain that whoever Julius Houghton was, he would soon be married to Florence Trefethen. After all, the man had proposed to her once. Florence only thought she knew men. Fargo knew better. When it came to women, men were damned foolish and easily led astray.

A little more wistfully than he cared to acknowledge, Fargo watched Florence's bustle bounce as she marched up the steps to the hotel. Then he ordered the hack driver to go on to Danielle DeLyon's parlor house.

Finding a whorehouse wasn't usually a problem, and the driver seemed to know just where it was. But the soap presentation was just breaking up when the hack passed that throng. The soap salesman spotted Fargo through the carriage window.

Aw, shit, Fargo thought as he saw that the tall whiskered gent was carrying a revolver, as well as a grudge for their little misunderstanding back in Denver. At the rate he was going, he was never going to get back to Charlie. A few days of lying down on the job, and everything seemed to have gotten out of control.

"Hey, you," the soap man shouted from thirty feet away as Fargo reached for his Colt. "You can't shoot my partners and live to tell about it."

"Want to bet on that?" Fargo shouted back, jumping from the moving hack. Crouching, he moved a dozen feet to the front of a saloon, where he'd have a brick wall behind him. No sense in having to worry about his back, especially when he didn't know how many allies the flimflam man might have, or where they might be lurking. Although the area had been crowded, people were scurrying out of the way.

The soap seller's first shot went high, about a foot over Fargo's head. The slug whined as it bounced off the brick, and the ricochet whistled just an inch over Fargo's shoulder. Fragments of shattered brick flew into the Trailsman's eyes.

Blinking furiously, Fargo fired back. His target was moving, and all he did was put a hole in one flapping tail of the man's hammer-prong coat. Besides, the gent had friends, one on each side, and they all had their guns out.

Shit. This was like a goddamn firing squad, except

he didn't have a blindfold. Not that it would have made much difference, the way his eyes were smarting as he tried to blink away the grit. Fargo dived forward. No sense just standing there and getting shot to pieces.

He landed with a splash in a mud puddle. At least the filthy water washed some of the crud out of his eyes. One bullet splatted into the mud, just next to his elbow, while the Trailsman got his Colt out in front of him.

Both hands on its grips, he got the hammer back and planted a slug in the soap-seller's chest. The man reeled back as blood poured down his linen shirt. But the other two didn't slow down; their bullets seemed as thick as that hail on the prairie.

No saddle to hide under, though. Fargo rolled, relying on his own powder smoke for cover. He got one man's shoulder, but it wasn't the man's gun hand, and he kept firing. The other one, though, gave up the instant that the Trailsman's slug plowed into his nose and emerged on the back side in a halo of red mist.

Jesus. The bastard that was still firing had managed to clip him. More than clip, although it was happenstance. His bullet had hit the standing water near Fargo's shoulder, flattened, and ricocheted right into the Trailsman's thigh, slicing wide.

Gritting away the pain, Fargo nailed the man's other shoulder. But he still didn't go down. Now he was holding that revolver with both hands, again bringing it up.

One bullet left, Fargo thought glumly. And his opponent had already taken two, and was still firing. Fargo lifted his head and fired his last round just as his opponent did. One round went low, skimming the street and throwing more grit into the Trailsman's eyes. The other was a bit low, too, slamming into the man's belly button instead of his chest, but it did the job.

After getting up and discovering that only one leg wanted to work, Fargo saw he couldn't avoid squaring this with the local law. Three uniformed policemen had appeared.

* * *

A week later, with stitches in his thigh, the Trailsman had decided that St. Louis ran a pretty fair jail. They'd treated him well, even to bringing in a doctor for his leg. As far as St. Louis was concerned, he'd done the city a favor in ridding them of the soap sellers. But he'd been wanted in Denver, and clearing that up required a court hearing before the judge agreed that the Trailsman had been right that time, too.

It was long past time to find Charlie and get that pup off to school. Fargo had fretted about the boy every day he'd been in jail, but he'd figured Charlie was fine. Although Fargo doubted Darius Hamilton would like having his boy schooled by Danielle DeLyon, worse things could have happened. On the other hand, the Trailsman couldn't remember ever having handled a job so poorly. But finding Charlie wasn't hard.

"Oh, Skye, zee young man, he is *très* enthusiastic," Danielle explained. "Zee ladies here, they like him so. And, *mon Dieu*, I do not know what I would do without him."

She'd taken Charlie over to her parlor house. The boy had taken to it like a duck to water, as any healthy male would. Of course he didn't have the money for sustained entertainment like that, but Danielle had quickly availed herself of the boy's aptitude for numbers.

He was keeping her books. Already she was making more money because he'd discovered how much her employees had been filching from her. He had watering drinks down to a science, and he'd figured out more subtle ways to rig the gambling downstairs. Charlie was even keeping track of all the money in circulation; in an instant, he could calculate how many Spanish doubloons or obscure Iowa bank notes it would take to equal a gold double-eagle of real American cash.

Fargo stepped out of Danielle's luxurious quarters and went down to Charlie's office. Smoking a big Havana cigar, the kid was going over some ledgers.

"Mr. Fargo, I like this. I thank you for all you've done, but I don't see a need to go to school."

"'Don't blame you for liking it. I'm kind of fond of

this life myself. But this ain't why I got you to St. Louis."

"Look, I've got me a good job. Leave me alone."

Fargo was of a mind to argue, but he heard footsteps padding on the thick carpet. He turned around and saw that he faced the two whorehouse bouncers. One was an immense black man, at least six feet six inches tall, with a mustache but a shaved head. The other was white and not quite as tall, but with arms the size of tree limbs, and shoulders to match.

His stitches reminded him that there were times to be discreet. Fargo rose slowly from his chair. "See you around, Charlie." He looked at the looming bouncers again. "I reckon I can find my own way out, if it's all the same to you."

Fargo stewed as he hobbled outside. Bad leg or not, he had to get Charlie out of Madame DeLyon's parlor house and over to the Covenant Academy, out on the edge of town. But it wouldn't do much good if the kid just ran away from school, back to the job he liked so much.

The Trailsman spent two days nosing around St. Louis, trying to round up some help among the seedy sorts he knew there. But he had an awful time explaining why he wanted to haul a boy out of a pleasant whorehouse and over to some snooty school. Fargo's acquaintances just laughed at the notion and wondered aloud if he was getting softheaded.

The kid hadn't just slipped off the straight and narrow. He was running off and eagerly sampling every delight that he was supposed to wait for. Fargo bitterly realized that he should have been more attentive. This was the last time he'd ever hire on as any sort of moral guardian. It just didn't come natural. It wasn't his line of work at all.

"Let's sort this out," the Trailsman muttered to himself while stepping out of his hotel room one morning. "Drinking and gambling and whoring are vices, sure enough, and best avoided until you're big enough to enjoy them properly. Kids like Charlie tend to think that the way you party on a Saturday night after a long trail ride is the way you ought to live all the time. But the absolute worst thing is not keeping your word. And I gave old Darius Hamilton my word that I'd get his boy to that school.

"You didn't get this far, through the opium and the gamblers and the Arapaho gals, and the dragging, and the hail, and the starvation and thirst, to give up now," he told himself as he made his way over to Madame DeLyon's in the cool of Monday morning. Hand on his Colt, he let himself in the back door. If he had to shoot it out with Danielle's entire payroll, he'd get Charlie out of there and over to school.

Whorehouses on Monday mornings were silent as tombs, although not nearly as neat. In the clutter of the main parlor, Charlie lay on an overstuffed couch, groaning and moaning. "Oh, shit," he asked the cushions, "why did I ever drink so much last night?"

He rolled over to see the Trailsman standing over him. "Mr. Fargo. Ohhh." He clutched his stomach.

"Some fresh air'll do you good, Charlie." He ignored the pain shooting along his leg to help the hung-over boy up. None of the bouncers appeared, so they shuffled through the back door without incident. All the while, Charlie reeled and tried to sound grown-up. "Those fancy gals. They can sure wear out a man," he complained.

He settled into the seat of the hack while Fargo told the driver to head out Chouteau Avenue to the academy.

They were almost there when Charlie pulled his head up and asked where they were headed.

"To school, Charlie," Fargo answered. "Looks like you've had all of the sporting life you can handle."

The boy started to reply, but then stuck his head out and got rid of whatever had been in his stomach. "Maybe you're right," he finally answered. "Don't know how much more of it I could take. I'm so tired."

"You think you're tired?" Fargo said, sinking back against the plush seat. It was the first time since leaving Gouge-Eye with Charlie that he'd really relaxed. "I've been plotting and planning and fretting on getting you out of that whorehouse night and day. This guardian business just isn't my line. I've been so worried I've pretty near decided I'll never risk having a boy of my own."

"Worried?" Charlie mused. "But, Mr. Fargo, I was perfectly safe with Miss DeLyon."

"A parlor house isn't a fitting place for a boy," Fargo objected.

"Why? Were you worried about my morals, Mr. Fargo?"

"Morals?" Fargo scoffed. "Hell, what do I know about morals?"

Fargo turned to look out the window. The huge mansions of the St. Louis aristocracy loomed behind fence and foliage. Fargo sighed.

"I'm a trailsman," he muttered. "I guide people, cattle, and wagons. I build roads into the wilderness. You're a smart kid, Charlie. You could build roads, bridges, railroads, anything you want. Maybe that's immoral. Changing the land that way. Bringing folks into the wilderness. But at least when I look back, I've done things for myself. That's got to be better than lining Dandy's pockets."

Wondering who in hell he thought he was to be giving the boy lectures, Fargo studied Charlie intently. It had to be pretty obvious to the boy that the Trailsman knew Dandy DeVine DeLyon Carmina all too well.

"Oh, hell, I don't know," Fargo confessed. "Maybe I'm wrong. You going to go running back to Dandy's the minute I'm gone?"

"You wouldn't like that, would you?" Charlie asked softly.

"No," Fargo admitted. "Your pa wouldn't like that either."

"Well, I can't say I'm real excited about school," Charlie reflected sadly. "But I wouldn't want to disappoint you or my dad." The boy straightened his shoulders and he looked considerably less dissipated, although he still didn't look real good. "I'll stay at the school," he promised. "And I'll study, too."

Getting Charlie to the school wasn't much trouble compared to getting him into the school. The Covenant Academy consisted mostly of two three-story brick buildings, set amid lawns and trees. One held most of the classrooms, and the other was a dormitory.

They walked up the steps in front of the classroom building, since it held the main office. That is, Fargo walked. Charlie still staggered. Then they had to navigate down a long hall with a slick, waxed hardwood floor. The boy only slipped twice before they turned another corner and found the office.

Miss Marguerite Carswell wore her gray hair in a bun and looked at them through gold-rimmed spectacles. She only came up to their shoulders, but the headmistress seemed to be looking down her nose at them, even after she got seated behind her desk.

"I am aware," she huffed, "that we were supposed to enroll young Master Hamilton for this term. But I could hardly admit a young man who is so far gone in debauchery. Why, he reeks of perfumed jezebels and the vile fumes of demon rum."

Charlie wasn't in any shape to say anything, and before Fargo could much more than open his mouth, she turned on him. "And you, Mr. Fargo. What sort of guardian have you been? Mr. Hamilton wrote that you would be escorting his son, and then I read in the newspapers of your shooting escapades with confidence men on the waterfront. I can see no reason now to admit Charles Hamilton to the Covenant Academy."

"Try this, lady." Fargo brought up the Colt and aimed it at the bridge of her spectacles. "Hear me. I am meaner than sin and I kill men for breakfast. I consort with wicked women, I whoop with the wild Indians in war parties, and I've taken a scalp or ten in my time. If you want this boy to turn out just like me . . ."

Miss Carswell smiled, although it looked like it might break her face. "I see your point, Mr. Fargo." She huffed some more. "Very well, then, we shall enroll him. But let me warn you that he must abide by our regulations. Which means no further recurrences of his current shameful condition."

Fargo holstered the Colt and eased Charlie into a chair before the kid fell down. "That's just fine by me, ma'am."

However far Charlie had strayed, the thin-lipped Miss Carswell obvious ran a tight ship. The kid would damn well behave himself henceforth.

The Trailsman's bootsteps echoed in the empty corridor as he left the school. Abruptly, the sound of running resonated behind him and he turned.

"Hey, Mr. Fargo, wait," Charlie yelled, skidding to a precarious stop before hurtling into the Trailsman. "I wanted to say good-bye."

Fargo nodded. "Me too. It's been right interesting." Feeling awkward, Fargo patted Charlie on the shoulder and turned to go. The boy followed him outside.

"I think it's been real interesting, too," Charlie called out as Fargo neared the waiting hack. "And Mr. Fargo," Charlie added, "I won't tell that old biddy, but I hope I turn out just like you."

The Trailsman turned. "You just might." Fargo laughed. "And all I can say is, I hope that's good."

LOOKING FORWARD!

**The following is the opening
section from the next novel in the exciting
Trailsman series from Signet:**

THE TRAILSMAN #80
BLOOD PASS

*1860, the edge of the Bitterroot Mountains,
a land still part of the Oregon Territory
but called Idaho by Indians, missionaries,
fur trappers, and all who braved
its untamed fierceness . . .*

The big man's eyes snapped open at the sound.

But he lay very still in the woodland glen, senses alert. Unmoving, he let his wild-creature hearing define the sound, let it take shape and form. It wasn't a raccoon, marten, or possum—no small creature. The steps were too heavy for a deer. An elk or a moose, he reasoned, and instantly corrected the thought. The steps were not cautious enough. He continued to listen and pursed his lips. A horse, with a rider. A horse moved differently without someone on its back.

Slowly he pushed himself up on one elbow, the big colt in his hand. He peered through the brush. The early-morning mists still hugged the ground, wispy trails, not unlike a giant, frayed scarf. It was unusually warm for October—Indian summer, most folks called it. He called it one of Mother Nature's tricks. The horse appeared, legs enshrouded by the mist, looking as though it were floating along the ground. He saw the rider and stiffened. A frown swept across his brow. He rubbed one big hand across his eyes and peered through the early morning again, wondering whether the mists had played tricks on him.

But they hadn't, and Skye Fargo felt astonishment sweep through him again. The rider was a girl. That didn't amaze him. He'd seen girl riders in the early morning before. But this one was stark-naked, absolutely and totally nude. He stared at her slender and shapely body—small, perfect breasts, beautiful legs, a flat stomach, and long, slightly scraggly blond hair around a face that seemed hardly more than fifteen. She rode bareback, appropriately enough. He grunted and stayed transfixed as she disappeared into the forest, still moving with slow, airy deliberate.

"Damn," Fargo swore softly, and pushed to his feet. He pulled on clothes, tossed his bedroll over the magnificent Ovaro with the jet black fore- and hindquarters and gleaming white midsection. He swung onto the horse and moved through the forest after the girl. The dewy morning grass clearly showed the marks of her horse's steps and Fargo followed the trail through the woods until he hurriedly reined up at the edge of a small cleared space around a tiny forest pond. The girl rested on a stone at the edge of the pond, an unruly lock of blond hair hanging over her face. she put her head back, her eyes half-closed, thin arms stretched out for support. Her small breasts were perfectly shaped little white mounds, each piquantly peaked with a very light-pink tip.

She was like an elfin creature who had suddenly emerged from a forest bower, a wood sprite that might vanish if he tried to approach closer. His eyes flicked to the horse and he saw an old mare with knobs on her knees and a coat that badly needed brushing. Nothing elfin about the horse, he grunted, and brought his eyes back to the girl. She leaned to one side, both breasts dipping beautifully, pulled up a blade of grass, and sucked on it with Cupid's-bow lips that made her face suddenly sensuous in a strange girl-woman way. Fargo slid silently from the Ovaro and stepped into the cleared space. The naked wood sprite looked up, light-blue eyes neither frightened nor particularly startled. "Hello," he said.

"Hello," she answered, her voice thin. She remained unmoving and met his stare as though she were fully clothed, and he felt himself frowning.

"That's quite a riding outfit," he remarked.

"My favorite," she said with a smile that managed to be both shy and suggestive.

"You always ride around like that?" he asked.

"At this hour, here in the woods," she said. "It's wonderful. You feel free and natural, like being one with everything in the forest."

He studied her, and her light-blue eyes returned his appraisal. She had a way of seeming as simple as a child and as wise as a woman, a combination he realized was very exciting. "You have a name?" he asked.

"Cassie," she murmured, and her eyes continued to appraise him. "What's your name?" she asked with direct simpleness.

"Fargo, Skye Fargo," he said. "You ever think you could get into trouble riding around like that?"

"You're the first person I've ever met at this hour of the morning," she said. "I've often wondered what I'd do if I did meet someone." She smiled and the smile held a sensuous pixiness in it.

"Doesn't seem to bother you any talking to me like that," Fargo commented.

"Does it bother you?" she asked slyly.

"Maybe," he allowed.

Her smile widened. "Good, because I suddenly want to make love, right here and now," Cassie said.

Fargo's gaze narrowed at her. "You often get these sudden urges?" he asked.

She shrugged, sat up straighter, and her breasts seemed to dance. "You think I shouldn't talk this way," she said with a sudden half-pout, suddenly child-like again.

"Didn't say that," Fargo returned.

She stood up, held her girl-woman body very straight,

slender legs slightly spread, flat little belly thrust forward, a small but very black triangle a sharp contrast to her milk-white skin. Again she seemed almost unreal, a woodland mirage. "It'd be natural, completely natural and simple, the way it ought to be," she said. "Don't you feel it, Fargo? Doesn't it reach you?"

"Something sure as hell is reaching me, honey," Fargo said, and he stepped toward her, his loins throbbing.

She took a step backward and lowered herself to the grass, her smile radiating girl-woman bewitchment. She lay back, stretched the nymphlike body, arms raised over her head as he pulled off clothes. Never turn away from something just because you don't expect it, he reminded himself as he dropped to his knees beside her. She brought her thin arms down, encircling his neck as he lay half over her and felt the smooth, soft babylike warmth of her skin. He bent his face down, took one small, peaked breast in his mouth, circled his lips around the light-pink tip, and felt her slender legs move under him.

"Don't wait. Now, now," she murmured to his surprise. He shifted himself over her. Both of her hands clasped his head, palms flattened against his temples, sliding down to his face, all but covering his ears. He felt her slender, flat-bellied body thrust up against him as she continued to clasp his face. He never heard the blow that crashed against the back of his head, but he felt her hands still half over his ears and then the sharp, shooting pain as the world went dark.

Dimly he felt himself being pushed to the ground, and tried to struggle to his knees in the black void. Another sharp burst of pain shot through him, then he felt only blankness, the utter void of time, place, and feeling.

He didn't know how long he'd lain there, but the pain returned with a slow, tickling sensation. He wondered how pain could tickle. Yet it did, in its own way, moving through his fingers, up his arms, spotting his legs. He forced his eyes open and let the world slowly take shape, become trees, leaves, branches. He started to sit up and cried out at the bolt that shot through the back of his head. He lay back again, his eyes open, cheek against the coolness of the grass. The pain slowly became bearable and he sat up once more.

He looked around and recognized the tiny pond and the stone. But the girl, the elfin wood sprite, was gone. So was nearly everything else. His gun, gun belt, clothes and boots had vanished. He peered at the Ovaro. His saddle was gone, along with all his gear and the big Sharps in its saddle case. He rose, winced, and straightened up as rage pushed pain aside. He had been drawn into a trap, led into it with a ploy no man could resist. "Wood sprite," he muttered aloud. "Bushwhacking little bitch." He walked to the Ovaro and pulled himself onto the horse, instantly feeling the warmth of the fur and hide against his buttocks and legs.

He glanced up at the sun. He'd been out for the better part of the morning, so he spurred the Ovaro forward, his eyes like ice as they scanned the ground. Suddenly he appreciated the warmth of Indian summer as he found the tracks of the girl's horse and followed the trail. He reined to a halt where she had stopped, and he saw additional hoofprints. By skirting the spot, he saw where they had ridden off together. There had been at least three horses, perhaps four; their prints were too close together to be sure.

They had stayed in the forest for a while, but eventually the prints emerged onto flat plains and led straight toward Ridersville. Fargo reined up. He had planned to make Ridersville himself before dusk, but that was when he had clothes. He turned the pinto around and went back into the trees. He dismounted inside the treeline and grimaced at his nakedness as he stared into the horizon. Maybe he could sneak into town in the dead of night and find something to wear. He pondered this but immediately discarded the thought. Ridersville was the kind of gateway town that never slept. There'd be no chance to sneak in stark-naked, not at any hour. Besides, he reminded himself, he hadn't a cent with which to buy a pair of Levi's. Damn that little wood-nymph bitch, he swore silently.

But if she and her friends had ridden into Ridersville, there was a good chance it was to sell his saddle—and everything else. He had to follow the trail, but first he had to find some clothes. He lowered himself onto a smooth rock and settled down, waiting and gazing across the plains that spread in front of him. A woman driving a buckboard went by in the distance. A half-hour later, four cowhands turned and headed toward town. Just as he'd decided to ride the pinto farther along the perimeter of the trees, a Conestoga moved slowly from left to right in the distance, silhouetted by the setting sun. He watched the lone wagon roll across the plains toward the foothills of the Beaverhead range in the far distance. As the sun lowered, the wagon grew dim and finally disappeared in the shroud of night.

If they were headed toward the Beaverhead range, he knew they'd have to camp for the night. When the moon rose he climbed onto the pinto and rode from the trees. Indian summer was a daytime event, he took note as he felt the chill of night on his naked body. He scanned the ground, easily picking up the wagon-wheel marks until he spotted the Conestoga pulled off at the edge of the trees. A lamp was still hanging from the front of the wagon, so he veered the Ovaro into the trees until he was closer to the wagon. He dismounted, crouched, and waited. Finally an arm reached out from the front of the wagon and took the lamp inside. Minutes later, the light went out and Fargo settled down to wait again. Everyone had to be asleep when he went to the wagon. When the moon was almost overhead, he crept to the rear corner of the old Contestoga.

He moved on catlike steps and pulled up one corner of canvas to peer into the back. He frowned as he saw two steamer trunks and a stack of hatboxes atop them.

His eyes went to the top edge of the canvas but he saw no clothes hanging to dry overnight. The trunk would be impossible to move in silence, so he reached for the top hatbox. It was large enough to hold more than a hat, and he carefully slid it toward him. He had it half out of the opening in the canvas when a voice snapped from the dakrness.

"Drop that box or I shoot."

Fargo flung himself sideways and rolled on the grass as he let the box topple to the ground. He came up behind the team of horses and crouched there as the figure swung to the ground from the tail of the Conestoga. A thin ray of moonlight showed brown, shoulder-length hair and a long robe that reached to the ankles. The woman moved closer and he saw the big Hawkins in her hands. She was young, with good, even features in her face, attractive even in the pale light of the half-moon. "Come out here where I can see you," she ordered.

"I don't think you want that," Fargo said. "I don't have a stitch on."

"Good try," she sniffed. "Now you get out here or I come after you shooting."

Fargo shrugged and moved away from the horses. He caught her quick hissed gasp of surprise as she stared at him. "Told you so, honey," he said.

"Get behind the horses again," she ordered, but he saw her glance linger at every part of his muscled body. He moved behind the rump of the nearest horse and saw that she kept the rifle level at him.

"I was trying to get some clothes," Fargo said.

"What happened to yours?" she asked.

Fargo grimaced. "You're not going to believe this," he said.

"Try me," she answered, so he took a deep breath and began to recount his misadventure, starting from the moment he'd first seen the blond wood sprite riding naked through the morning mists. He drew another deep breath when he finished.

"Told you you wouldn't believe me. Can't say I blame you," he said.

Her eyes peered at him for another moment. "I believe you," she said.

"You do?" he blurted. "Why?" he asked out of astonished curiosity.

"That story's too damn wild to make up and use," she said. "It has to be true."

Fargo managed a smile. "You're very sharp," he said. "And I'm glad for that. The whole thing's made me feel like a damn fool."

"Serves you right," she sniffed, and he frowned back. "But then you're all the same, always panting to please yourselves."

"I don't believe in passing up opportunities," he said.

"Even a mouse knows to sniff around before he grabs a piece of cheese," she tossed back disdainfully.

Skye swore silently at the truth of her sharpness. "I still need some clothes," he grumbled, and she finally lowered the big Hawkins.

"Just so happens I'm on my way to meet up with some other wagons. I'm bringing supplies, lots of different things," she said, casting another appraising glance at his chest and shoulders. "You're big, but I've got some things that might fit well enough," she said, and quickly climbed back into the Conestoga. She turned on a lamp and he saw her shadow rummaging through boxes. Finally she leaned out and tossed him a pair of trousers, a jacket, and two dirty boots. He sat down and pulled them on. The boots fit best, for the trousers barely closed and the jacket was drawn tight across his chest. She gazed at him when he stepped from the horses.

"They'll do," he said. "Much obliged."

"Some of my brother's things."

Fargo threw a glance at the wagon. "But you're alone," he said.

"Until I join the other wagons," she answered.

"If you tell me where, I'll try to get these back to you," he said.

"No need, really. They're extras," she said. "But we're meeting at Beaverhead, alongside the Madison."

"What do you know? The world's full of coincidences," Fargo said. "I was heading that way myself. Maybe I will be able to get these things back to you."

She shrugged. "We won't be staying there long," she said.

"What's your name, 'case I get there in time," he said.

"Hope Maxwell," she said. "You're welcome to bed down here. I've an extra blanket and the night wind's getting sharp."

He thought for a moment. Chances were he'd find out little in Ridersville in the middle of the night and would have to wait for morning, anyway. "I'd be obliged again," he said, and this time she stepped from the wagon and brought him the blanket. She had round brown eyes, slightly rounded cheeks, and a short nose with a little tilt to the end of it. It was a very attractive face. "Tell me one thing." He smiled. "I'm usually too quiet for most folks to hear. How'd you pick up I was moving that hatbox?"

"I was awake the whole time. I knew I was being followed from the moment I settled down for the night," she said. His eyes questioned her. "Call it a sixth sense," she said. "I've always had it, a kind of inner knowing. More than intuition. It scares me sometimes."

He nodded, and her brown eyes held his for a moment longer.

"Good night," she said and climbed into the wagon.

He smiled as he lay down with the blanket just beside the wheels. She hadn't asked his name. It was a strange passing incident and she'd make no more of it. There was a determination under her acuteness. She was on her way to a rendezvous and she'd not let herself be drawn into any detours, no matter how intriguing they might be. But she'd been generous and he was grateful to her. He closed his eyes and sleep came to him at once.

Only the sharp bark of prairie dogs interrupted his slumber. The wagon was still and he rose, folded the blanket, and pulled aside a part of the canvas flap at the tail gate. She lay asleep on a mattress on the wagon floor, her brown hair falling loosely around her face. Her cheeks were rounder in the light of dawn than they'd seemed in the moonlight shadows, she was prettier. But even asleep, the determination was in her face, and he silently backed from the wagon, climbed onto the Ovaro, and sent the horse at a slow walk across the plains.

He rode with his lake-blue eyes hardening, the line of his jaw growing tight. Chasing down a blonde, bushwhacking wood nymph was a first for him, he grunted. But he'd sure as hell chase her down.

DOUBLE BARRELED ACTION!